# FOREBEAR

A NOVEL

MARSHALL GADDIS

SHIVAREE
PUBLISHING
BUTTE MT 59701

Shivaree Publishing
121 N. Main Street
Butte MT 59701
shivareepublishing.com

REGISTERED TRADEMARK—MARCA REGISTRADA

SHIVAREE
PUBLISHING



Ordering Information:
Discounts are available for quantity purchases. For details, contact the publisher.

Forebear / Marshall Gaddis — 1st ed.
ISBN 978-0-9981646-0-1

*for Renee*
*with love*

FOREBEAR

*He was scourged, put to the rack, his body torn with hooks, his flesh cut with knives, his face scarified, his teeth beaten from their sockets, and his hair plucked up by the roots... He was struck by lightning so as to fall to the ground... and this affected him so sensibly that, without communicating his purpose to any of his friends, he withdrew himself from the world.*

— *William Gaddis, The Recognitions*

*Fear no more the heat o' the sun,*
*Nor the furious winter's rages;*
*Thou thy worldly task hast done,*
*Home art gone and ta'en thy wages*
— *William Shakespeare, Cymbeline*

*I will follow the white man's trail. I will make him my friend, but I will not bend my back to his burdens. I will be cunning as a coyote. I will ask him to help me understand his ways. Then I will prepare the way for my children, and their children. The Great Spirit has shown me. A day will come when they will outrun the white man in his own shoes.*

— *Many Horses, Oglála Lakota medicine man,*
*when the last Ghost Dance failed at Standing Rock*

# CONTENTS

# PROLOGUE

## OCTOBER 1825

Scores settled, wounds healed as much as ever they would, the old trapper broke camp a month early and set off back to Fort Kiowa before snows got fierce. Weather sense said this winter'd come on quick.

Figured he'd stick it out just long enough to sell off his plews and make sure they got shipped down to St. Louis before the Missouri iced over. Then light out for high country where pelts'd grow lush and nobody'd be around to stumble on his traplines or fuss him otherwise.

But barely had he arrived at the trading post and sat down to some grub before he got cornered by a damn journalist who introduced himself as Hubert Somebody before asking, "And who might you be?"

"Hugh Glass," said the trapper.

The newspaperman stared at Hugh's scars. "Jumping Jehosophat." He offered his hand and said, "An honor, Mr. Glass. I never expected..."

Hugh Glass ignored the paw, not much on touching people.

The newspaperman said, "Hugh, Hubert. We nearly have something in common, Hugh, if I may call you that."

Glass looked him up and down: pale, thin under a snapbrim hat and city overcoat buttoned to the neck, wearing stiff new military brogans so heavy he'd fall behind in the woods and never make it through the swamps. Left and right boots built from the same last'd take forever to break in. Forever to dry.

"Moccasins," Glass said.

"Pardon?" Hubert said.

"Moccasins," Glass said.

"Pardon?"

"Get you some. Shed them clodhoppers you're shod in. Blisters. Trenchfoot."

"I welcome wilderness advice, sir. Yours especially. Might we talk awhile? Came all this way for a fur trade story but these trappers seem unwilling to converse. Could make one or two famous if they'd allow it."

"Got my permission," Hugh Glass said.

"Can't write you up much more," the reporter said. "Who doesn't know about you and the bear? Your crawling all those miles to get your rifle and your knife and your revenge? I'm gratified to see you looking hale and hearty but that's not much more than a paragraph. You already have your fame."

"Some's good, more's better," Glass said.

Only part of fame he cared about was the guide money he made after spring breakup once keelboats could travel this far upriver. Each year he'd slouch against a cottonwood as Easterners disembarked. One look at his bear-clawed face, somebody'd figure him for the penny press legend. Word would spread like wildfire. Quickest among them would ask was he available. By sundown he'd sign up two or three excursions, maybe an expedition or two. That night he'd prowl around with a bottle to share with experienced hands, see who was available or expected and sign on the best.

"'Fraid you're not still news," Hubert said. "No tale I send back about you now can top what's been said. I can work you into a story, sure, maybe how you're teaching newcomers to survive. Like that Bridger kid. Soon as I saw him I knew my readers'd eat up every word about a fellow that young in the fur trade. 'Cause, see, every farm boy or clerk'd be thinking that could be him having adventures, what it'd be like if he had the guts to light out, and every milkmaid'd be wishing for someone like him to ride into her life. Asked him a question or two just now but he goggled at me like I was something in a circus. Walked off without manners enough to say word one."

"Galoots hereabouts don't hold manners in high regard. Words either, that matter. Few can read. Most barely write their own names."

"You, sir, are reputed to be a man of letters."

"Schooled a bit growing up," Glass admitted. "Only letters I have truck with these days are ones to parents or sweethearts of some man's hair's been lifted."

"Got to admit, though, that galoot's a word not often heard. Seafaring term, I believe."

Hugh Glass, silent, glimpsed where this Hubert fellow was headed. Clear as a badger trail in the snow. Tell you there's no story to be had just as he's sneaking up on one.

"Some have it you were a sailor in your younger years," the journalist said, leaning close. Glass whiffed a powdery scent over the stink of all the other two-leggeds in the place.

"Cut my teeth as a mariner," Glass said.

Hubert flipped open a morocco-bound notebook, pulled a stick of wood from his pocket. "True you were a pirate with Jean Lafitte?"

"Privateer," Glass said, "not pirate. American navy hired us. Sink enemy ships. Spaniards, then Englishmen."

Hubert scribbled in his notebook.

"What kind of pen is that?" Glass said.

"None, sir. It's called a pencil. Make them up toward Boston."

"Where's the ink?"

"Requires none."

Hubert handed him the cedar stick.

Glass peered at the pointed black cone in the center and dragged it across the palm of his hand. "It don't write."

"Try it on something dry. Paper's my preference." Hubert baiting him with a little sarcasm, maybe slyer'n he seemed.

Glass reached for the notebook, drew a line and marveled at it.

"Sign your name," the dandy said. "I'll hang onto your autograph."

Glass handed him back the pencil and the unsigned book.

Hubert said, "But they weren't all warships were they? Y'all captured cargo ships too."

"Ordered to keep provisions out of the hands of the enemy," Glass said.

"That you retained, am I correct? Or sold at a profit?"

Old Glass favored brisk replies over running off at the mouth. "You seem mighty well informed, someone so far away from where it happened. Is it the writer's trade, invent what he don't know or understand?"

Hubert's mouth pooched out with replies of his own, looking undecided which one to spit out.

"Spoils of war," Glass continued. "Turned it all over to Jean and his one-eyed brother, tote it all up, portion out our share. It was them financed our sorties so we tithed."

"Including slaves sometimes?"

"Ever' once in a while."

"Did that bother you?"

"No end of things was bothering me."

Talking and scrawling more quickly now but still shooting him a bored look, Hubert flipped a page with his thumb. "How'd you come to be working for pirates in the first place?"

"Same way's we all did. Their broadsides disabled our vessel. We was boarded and looted and scuttled. Go along with 'em or go under. Take the oath or die."

"But later you could quit?"

"Didn't call it that. Called it mutiny. Take your chances on a drum-head court-martial. Pirates not noted for their deliberations but only Lafitte could give the nod to a gibbeting. If not, you're oared ashore. Handshakes all around and a by-your-leave."

Hubert smiled. "So you did what? Details. Readers need details."

"Timed it right. Said nothing. Waited for a big victory. We was anchored just leeward of Campeche and the crew got shore leave."

"Who's we? I was under the impression you escaped alone and only came by a companion somewhere along the way."

"Cap'n Forrest. Generally well-liked so nobody bothered to lock us below. They was in a real hurry to rouse Lafitte from his Maison Rouge featherbed with the news so's they could head on out to piss away their cut. Figured we'd keep until morning."

"And you didn't?"

"Stuck around long enough to make sure the crew was carousing in the groggeries with their drink and their weed. Skeleton crew below with a hogshead. Moon behind the clouds, we give each other a look. Tore off our shoes and dove on in, just our clothes and what was in our pockets. Swam to the mainland and was off to the races."

"I've heard the tale," Hubert said, face stiff with disbelief. "You walked a long ways."

"Up across Spanish Texas into Missouri Territory. I was always a walking fool. Forrest kept up okay."

"But you were a sailor then, not the mountain man you are now."

"Liked hoofing all the same. Just not as much opportunity or such a good reason."

"Hundreds of miles without shoes? Without weapons?"

"No such thing's without. Ain't got 'em you make 'em. Pickings easy enough. Skunk pigs there so fierce you bait 'em with any grub at all or something with a smell might be grub, they come right at you, dare you do your worst. Grip you a stout mesquite branch, a big-assed rock lashed on for a war club. Well-sharpened stick in the other hand, you'll get you moccasins and food aplenty. Tusks don't curve like swine. Straight, broad enough to scrape hide, strong's a steel blade. Make great pigstickers or anything else needs sticking."

Hubert put his pencil down.

Old Glass couldn't blame the man. He'd scorn any such tall tale was spun at him. Made it up spur of the moment, never thinking word'd spread. Way too late to change it now. Raise questions. Way they'd abandoned the pirate life. What they did or didn't take. Where the plunder might be now.

Only three people knew the truth of that.

Couple of years, maybe, Lafitte brothers die off the way they should and their pirates disband, he'd find some other Hubert to juice up the Hugh Glass legend. But only after he and Forrest snuck back for the buried loot.

"Guess that's when you were captured by Indians," Hubert said, maybe faking some extra boredom.

"Wolf Pawnee."

"Burnt your partner at the stake, story goes."

"Not the way you might suppose," Glass said. "Indians wouldn't waste the wood. Damn few big trees where they roamed. Took his clothes and poked hundreds of dry twigs into Forrest. All his parts. Set the sticks on fire. Hard a way to die's there is, I reckon."

"You watched him burn?"

"Till they was all looking his way. Got real busy real fast."

"Some sort of warpaint, newspaper accounts said."

"Cinnabar powder. Had a tin in my pocket. I wasn't tied up or nothing 'cause they was going to do me next and would just as lief I tried to run. Scooped me out a little handful. Pissed on it. Smeared up my cheeks real good. Pesky turned around, it give him a fright. Let out a shout then they all did. Figured me some kind of spirit had so much magic my face turned to flame soon's Forrest's did."

"Odd thing to have in your pocket, carried all that way. Would've thought swimming'd've ruined it."

"Those tins was tight. Always kept 'em to store fixin's to make a fire."

"Why then still keep the powder?"

"Every sailor did for shore leave. Often's not hoors'd trade to rouge themselves up."

"But you were miles from, um, ladies of that sort. Frontier territory."

"May not be the man of the world you are," old Glass said. "But I spent me some time with Pawnees and others. Ain't never seen a woman won't daub her face up some."

"Just surprised you thought that far ahead when you grabbed what you could, jumped off your ship, carried it so long."

"Don't see it's so surprising. Indians like face paint, not just the women. Best trade goods ever. Easier'n carrying whiskey or muskets. Harder to come by'n beads. Deeper red than berry juice and if you're riding down an enemy don't come off from rain or sweat. Why you think call 'em redskins?"

Hubert was back to making a few notes. "The story is they took you in? Made you a member of the tribe?"

"Believed my magic'd bring 'em luck. Lived in the chief's lodges a couple of years. Hunted buffalo together'n the occasional Cheyenne or Sioux. Learned to set snares. Fight'n ride'n attack'n escape. Taught me survive some pretty harsh land. Stood me in good stead as you know."

"As don't we all? Can we go back to the pirates? My readers'd have more interest."

"Thought you was writing about the fur trade. Why you want to know all that?"

"Sometimes," Hubert said, "you don't get the story you want but stumble on a better one. Even in Europe, you say mountain man, you're the first one comes to mind. Everybody's heard your time with the Indians and all that came after. Your early sailor and pirate years is just a rumor. Might well be the better tale."

"Freebooter, not pirate," Glass said. "One of many. No story to be had there but the one I just give you."

He stood, gathered his kit and lit out for the door. Get back in that cold, clean air.

# CHAPTER ONE

# ASSKICK

Pumped up music blares Natty's fighter, Brendan "Bear" Glass, through the tunnel and down HP Pavilion's strobe-lighted runway. He's hunched low slapping outstretched fan-hands, low-fiving their high-fives.

On the dressing room's bigscreen a shaveheaded play-by-play announcer cageside and his color guy recap the usual cliches about Brendan the Bear: legendary back in the day, dropped from the UFC following several straight losses, snapped up by their cable network hot to get in on the action and the demographic.

Tons of experience, always dangerous, glad to take a fight on short notice. Got his nickname a decade ago from his oversized head, powerful arms and shoulders merging into a long torso without the interruption of a neck; short, stocky legs that stalk opponents across the cage;

the low center of gravity that makes him so hard to take down; his take-no-prisoners style.

The commentator rambles on, filling empty air until the fight starts. He says something about Glass's physiognomy. Color guy dives in like a good sport, says fizzy-what?

In the dressing room Natty finishes grinding up some Vitamin K with the bottom of an empty coumadin bottle. He tears open a packet of powdered energy drink and mixes the two together. He fills a sports bottle with water and pours in the powder with a bartender shake that foams it into a witch's potion.

The cage announcer steps up to the boom mic to introduce the fighters, Natty's cue to tote the bottle down the aisle and take his seat near Brendan's cornermen.

The ref takes it from there. "Fighters, *are* you ready? You ready? *You* ready? Bring it on, c'mon."

The first round goes according to plan. Bear Glass keeps shambling in but shambling fast, relentless as long as he can keep his steam up, throwing vicious powerhouse punches the young Brazilian mostly manages to avoid, backing away, maintaining his distance.

The Bear's loyal fans cheer him on and he's giving them a show, throwing jabs and legkick after legkick, attempting takedowns, swinging for the fences.

His conditioning's pretty good for his age but by the end of the round he's breathing through his mouth and his hands are dropping.

At the buzzer his opponent ambles back to the blue corner as if he's been taking his bitch for a stroll in the park.

Round two. Ringbabes parade outside the cage, hoisting numbered placards angled toward the audience. As if anybody out there's looking at the cards. Ladies spend way more time in the gym than Brendan, who at the bell sidles away from the red corner knowing what he's in for. Only a fool would take this fight on two weeks' notice after the scheduled opponent dropped out from a torn training-camp ACL.

It's the Brazilian's first U.S. fight so Brendan's got no tapes to study. Not that he's ever changed his strategy much for an opponent anyway. What he does know, the dude has youth on his side and a reach advantage. Moved to the States to train with American Top Team after giving the Blackzilians a good look. Local favorite tonight except for Brendan's old fans and the shouting clump of bikers he used to ride with.

Brendan advances to the center of the cage, watchful. How's it going to play out this time? He holds his body in a long C-curve, one hamfist cocked by his right ear and his left extended to grab or jab.

The rangy Brazilian stutter-steps and then comes at him with a Jose Aldo flying knee that Brendan's chin barely avoids. A follow-up roundhouse kick takes his left leg out from under him.

He's busy regaining his balance when a spinning back-elbow connects. Brendan feels blood jetting over his face. The scartissue above his brow must've split.

The Brazilian backs off with a smile, mission accomplished, and starts to play for the crowd. He methodically takes Brendan apart, darting in and out with every combination he's got, obeying numbers and Portuguese codewords shouted in from his corner.

Brendan gets no chance to counterpunch, much less let fly his trademark looping right. Inside kicks smash his leading knee and thigh, deadening his footwork. Jabs and headkicks keep him from closing in.

Not much fun to be had from here on out but a paycheck's a paycheck. Brendan tries a couple of desperation takedowns but it's a running-through-molasses dream.

He's taken down twice himself and the elbows rain down on his face. A D'Arce choke almost finishes him but he escapes at the last minute. Gets his feet under him and wallwalks back up. Of course the guy's not really trying to stop him. The crowd prefers them on their feet slugging away and it's all about what the crowd prefers.

The Brazilian closes in for the kill with Muay Thai clinches and dirty boxing up against the cage, leaning into him and sapping his strength. Locks his hands behind Brendan's neck and launches knee after knee to the face.

Brendan's head is splitting open. He swipes blood away from his eyes with the back of his glove so the ref won't stop the fight.

The Brazilian goes to the body. Vicious kidney punches and solar plexus stabs leave him gasping and cramped.

Brendan takes a quick look at the clock. All that gets him is an overhand left to the gash, the guy of course targeting it.

Brendan hears something crack. Nothing up there should make that kind of noise. His vision starts troubling him immediately, and it's not just the blood.

Another bullrush pokes him back against the cage. The striking's relentless and he's run out of defense. The Brazilian could take him down at will and finish him with ground-and-pound but instead milks the round for all it's worth. Brendan can barely see past the crimson mist but the cheering and screaming tell him the crowd's on its feet.

Hands back of his neck pull his face down again. Long legs he can't see to defend against come up at him. Another knee to the brow and he hears that cracking sound again.

Got to get out of this clinch. Can't stay standing. Brendan lets his legs fold so he can drop to the ground and take his chances there. But the Brazilian's holding him up with double underhooks and bad intentions.

Brendan covers his head with both forearms but it's still knee city.

He feels the ref separate them. Now he can fall and he does, hard. He pulls himself into a sitting position, hearing his blood splash on canvas, and protests to the ref, "I was defending myself. I can still fight."

"Not saving you from him, Bear. Saving you from you. What you need this for?"

His trainers get him to a stool where the cage doc works to stanch the blood, pressing and wiping away the scarlet haze that blossoms right back. Could use some windshield wipers.

Now here comes Natty into the cage. Which is weird; he never does that. Natty's pushing a sports bottle at him. "Drink it all, quick. Don't spit it out. It's your pick-me-up."

Brendan chugs the bottle before the cage doc swats it away and shoulders Natty aside. Brendan hears a fading shout. "Get me the Avitene. Get me the Thrombin. Something's not right."

# CHAPTER TWO

# WHIPPED

Laura Engebretson waits for her boyfriend Branch to come by her Hyalite condo a few blocks from the university. He's never on time but she usually doesn't mind. Always plenty to do.

This morning, though, she's pissed. Burned out from research and her dissertation, she wants nothing more than the quiet, uneventful weekend at his brokedick little ranch near Pony they'd planned. But yesterday he called to suggest they spend Saturday afternoon at Hampton's home instead. Give her a chance to size up the guy Branch wants to go into business with.

Watch them some college football, he said, and then the big fight on pay-per-view. Branch's uncle Brendan—they never call him Bear—is taking on some newcomer. He's actually a cousin but for years was the closest thing to a father Branch had, so Uncle Brendan is what he's always been called.

"Need to watch the fight from somewhere," Branch said. "Busy as you been, don't think it's right, drag you into some loud-ass bar for hours."

Her condo has no television and never will so she couldn't really say no. Branch has been touting Hampton as a big business asset with money made in real estate; wants to partner up. So she's wearing some nice boots and a newer pair of jeans to set off the scalloped sweater and matching scarf, slouch hat and opera-length fingerless mitts she had woven at Alpacas of Montucky just down the road.

She's a ranch gal. Some people don't like that word gal but she does. What else goes with ranch? Ranch girl? No. Ranch lady? Lady rancher? Maybe someday but not yet. She'll answer to cowgirl if she's in a rodeo ring or wearing one. But ranch gal says it all for someone born and raised in the Grasshopper Valley to roam the biggest red Angus spread in the state.

Now in her last semester of grad school, she's indoors more than she'd like. But not much else has changed. She's still footloose and makeup-free, certain that Angus history is about to take a quantum leap and she's just the gal to make it happen.

Her dissertation's almost done and she can't stand to look at it anymore. The Red Angus Association's website is up to date. So she looks at the clock, sighs, and starts the family blog, *History of the Tumbling E*, been in the back of her mind for months. With luck she'll get it done in time to parchment-print it and surprise her mom and dad for their thirtieth wedding anniversary.

The Tumbling E ranch first took shape in 1862. Montucky's first gold strike in Grasshopper Creek brought miners streaming up the Montucky Trail from Utah. The find was so rich and the gold so easy to obtain that soon ten thousand people had cobbled together a rough-hewn town of sorts. One of the first to arrive, a second-generation Norwegian named Einar Engebretson, filled his poke early and wondered what to do now that too many people were elbow-to-elbow along the creek, their sluice boxes and gold pans clanging against each other.

The crowds were a problem in another way. Men were scuffling for food almost as much as for gold. The town was too far from any supply of food or provisions. Pack trains and ox-wagons from the Great Salt Lake could only make three or four treks a year up the Montucky Trail. Nothing was fresh. There was one grocery store that mostly just carried salt, flour and whiskey. Two meat markets but no meat. Game was hard to come by since horses and mules were scarce.

So Engebretson bought a mare and started exploring upstream. Soon he came upon beautiful open pastureland with rich, alluvial soil at the foot of the Pioneer Mountains, a half-hour's ride from town.

Engebretson's family was back in Minnesota. Like most recent immigrants from Norway, they were farmers. He was able to get mail back to them by sending it overland to Fort Benton and then down the Missouri. He explained that all those half-starved men were an incredible opportunity and tried to coax the entire family out to join him.

At first they were reluctant. It was too far, too wild, and they'd invested five years in getting established in the Minnesota River Valley. Norwegians were moving into Minnesota in greater numbers so it felt like home. They wrote back about the Homestead Act passed by Congress the same year as the gold strike. In a move designed to open up Western settlement to individual families rather than big southern landholders who relied on slave labor, the law authorized any head of household over 21 who had not taken up arms against his country in the Civil War to settle 160 acres. After five years, if he'd improved the land, it would be deeded to him. The land rush was on and good farmland was going fast.

Engebretson was disappointed to have to go it alone, but a deed to 160 acres sounded good. Likely nobody else around here knew about the Homestead Act yet. He asked his relatives to send him more information and all the seeds they could spare. He figured most things that grew in Minnesota could grow here if they didn't require too much water.

Before the first snow fell he'd erected a small, serviceable log cabin, provisioned a root cellar with such food as he'd been able to procure in town, taken an elk and a doe, and received his seeds. With them came news of an Indian uprising in the Minnesota River Valley. Several Dakota Sioux tribes were infuriated that the annuities promised by treaty were being held by the Indian agents who were supposed to hand them out. They requested payments come directly to the tribes so they wouldn't have to buy supplies on credit from the white traders. The Indian agents refused and the traders stopped selling on credit. Hunger and anger rose.

The uprising started when a small Dakota hunting party crossed onto a settler's land and one of the four men saw a chance to steal a few hens' eggs. The settler came upon them with his rifle. Before he could kill them they killed him, and then four other settlers. That night a tribal council agreed to attack up and down the valley, drive away all white settlers and burn down their buildings so they wouldn't come back.

With over 20,000 able-bodied men serving in Minnesota cavalry and infantry regiments fighting on the Union side far away, there was little resistance. The Sioux overwhelmed the whites, killing hundreds of men, women and children in the first few months, sometimes in particularly horrible ways. One survivor described a pregnant woman being cut open, her unborn infant pulled from her and nailed to a barn. Settlers, many of them Norwegian, fled their blazing farmhouses.

The Engebretson clan lost a few lives and everything they'd worked for. The letter said they were on their way south to Iowa to take refuge with relatives for the winter. They'd all join Einar in the spring.

Engebretson told nobody in town about the Homestead Act. He quietly walked the valley, identifying the best farmland. There'd likely be five or six households coming. Including him, that'd be almost a thousand acres of free homestead. And if he selected adjoining parcels they could share grazing land for livestock.

Early the next spring the families started trickling in, having come by sidewheeler steamboat up the Missouri river from Fort Charles and then overland along the Yellowstone.

Soon he and all six families—along with three of their neighbors—worked alongside each other to build houses and barns for all, to irrigate and till and seed and water and cultivate vegetables and fruits.

Some of the neighbors had daughters. It wasn't long before Einar Engebretson set about fathering a family of his own.

Laura Engebretson powers down her computer. Still no word from Branch, so she refills her coffee cup and brews some green tea. Be damned if she's going to call and nag him.

An hour later he shows up. She rarely locks her door so he just gives it one good knock and comes on in.

Pretty dressed up himself, he hesitates, probably checking her mood, before pulling her to her feet. It's a long kiss and a good one.

"Nice," he says. "I was afraid you'd be mad."

"Mad?" Laura says. "Me? Because you're so late? Why should I care? It's your buddy and your deal, not mine."

"Let's go then. You ready? I don't want to miss the kickoff."

"Give me twenty minutes or so. I want to fix my hair."

"Honey—"

"I'm funning you. Of course I'm ready. My hair look like it needs fixing to you?"

"Mind if I tell Hamp it was you made me late?"

"Hell no. Long's you don't mind me telling him how full of shit you are."

"Sweet as ever."

They drive north of town in Branch's crewcab. As they enter lower Bridger Canyon, the countryside turns lush and the homes even more so.

Laura expects a real estate guy to have a big house but she's still kind of blown away when they turn through a double gate and up the sweeping driveway. It's a damn fortress, logs over granite. Even a turret.

The man who meets them in the atrium is halfway handsome in a smug, fortyish sort of way. His greeting seems sort of perfunctory but at least he's not oozing charm at her.

Laura scans the walls up to the cathedral ceiling for narrow gun embrasures. Maybe archers with longbows. Or somebody lurking on the roof with a pot of boiling oil.

They get the proud owner tour, one extravagance after another, and a wave of a hand to "the wife." That's about it for aboveground.

Hampton struts them down to his mancave, exuding fat cat, and ushers them past the pigroast fireplace where cast iron firedogs support three massive logs. The heat is so intense she gives it a wide berth, fearing scorched alpaca. Her dad likes to say, "Indian build small fire, sit close. White man build big fire, sit way back."

Hampton guides them past a turn-of-the-century backbar salvaged from a Tightsqueeze tavern and points them toward theatrical seating facing a huge flatscreen on the wall, centered between the moose mount and the mountain goat. JBL monitors and a subwoofer all too faithfully reproduce every detail of stadium crowdnoise and overwrought announcers. There's even a karaoke machine and two mics.

A few minutes of smalltalk include her before Hampton and Branch do the guy thing, beer-bonding over every subject except what they're really here for. She easily tunes out their chatter but can't overcome the surround sound and flicker of a couple of faraway teams that hold no interest.

The wife, accompanied by two unidentified daughters, or maybe it's a daughter and a friend, shuttle in silently with tasty hors d'oeuvres. Brittany, Hampton's wife, is trim and suburban, conventionally pretty and mighty well turned out for a Saturday at home. The two girls are a bit more relaxed, but on their best behavior.

Hampton doesn't introduce them so Laura strides over, presents herself and gets their first names. She asks what's in the delicacies and can she help.

Growing up on the ranch, football afternoons were always extended-family affairs. Neighbors and kids trooped in and out of the kitchen into the living room where the Griz or the Bobcats played their hearts out on the tall mahogany Philco. Doors always slamming. Four-wheelers and snowmobiles firing up outside, depending on the weather, and roaring off to chores or adventure. Dedicated fans—men, women, girls, boys and a dog or two—sprawled across worn chairs or couches. Beer and soda pop everywhere.

Women with any sense soon gravitated to the big farm kitchen to share in the work and enjoy the company. Refills of white wine and cooking sherry were easy to come by, soon as she was old enough to ask. Way better conversation where she learned what a Montucky teen-ager needs to know to carry on the ranching tradition.

No woman in Montucky ever turns down a request to help out. At least Laura's never heard of it happening. But that's what these ladies do. They go, "O no, no, we couldn't," hands all aflutter.

This isn't friends dropping by. This is some kind of business meeting. Instructions have been given.

At halftime Laura tries again. Heads upstairs for a bathroom but before she reaches the stairs she's admonished that there's one in the cave. Of course there is. It turns out to sport Gilded Age reproduction faucets and something on the wall she can't identify, a flush-mounted brushed steel compartment with a lid. It looks like a cross between a Venus flytrap and a pelican's pouch.

She investigates. Pushes a button and the lid glides up. It's the damnedest urinal she's ever seen. Looks like it could grab a man and pull him right in, start to digest him on the spot.

She keeps her distance from the contraption and does what she came for.

By the two-minute warning, the menfolk are jawing about duck-hunting, all but ignoring the game.

At the final whistle, Hampton hauls out a box of cigars. It's obvious he wants her to leave the room. At least she and Hampton have one thing in common.

The wife brings in a plateful of something she calls can-apes. They look mighty good. Laura presses for details. Seared Copper River sockeye salmon flown in yesterday, with leeks, morels and baby asparagus on artisan bread, all from the farmers' market. Brittany Hampton offers Laura the first one and then puts the platter on the coffee table in front of the men.

Laura bites in. "Wow," she says, her admiration real. "These couldn't be any more perfect. Wild-caught for sure. Wait. Don't go yet."

It's no time for subtlety. She stands, grabs a couple more off the tray in one hand and a couple of empty trays in the other, and leads the way to the stairs. "You've got to show me how you made these canapés," diplomatically offering up the language lesson. "Food's my strongest weakness."

Endless minutes later, out of the fire and into the frying pan, Laura is suffocating in a big designer kitchen hung with immaculate copper utensils. Seldom is heard an intelligent word as the women stand around uncomfortably making smalltalk, visibly wishing her away.

Finally Branch's shout reaches her. "Honey, come on down. Uncle Brendan's getting greased."

Greased? The fight's already started? She lopes down the stairs but it's just some functionary smearing vaseline over Brendan's forehead and brows. "Skin won't split so easily," Hampton says.

Laura shudders.

Brendan finishes the pre-fight inspection and bounds into the cage.

Before she met him last year, not long after she and Branch got serious about each other, Laura was sure she'd despise anyone who did what he did for a living. How could you call mixed martial arts a sport? Much less an art, or those brutes artists? Not even the pretense of a ball to carry or a puck to move down the ice.

The way Branch'd explained it to her, fighters made almost no money unless they survived to reach the heights Brendan had. But the promoters made out like bandits. To her, it was all just a scam, glorifying the most brutish aspects of the male subspecies by stoking and stroking the bloodlust of these eager young guys and even older ones like Brendan.

Brendan called Branch one December day to say he had enough time between fights to book a ski vacation at Big Sky. He invited them both to join him for a week at the condo his sponsor was renting for him. He'd cover the costs of meals, entertainment and lift tickets. It would be a good, relaxing way to get acquainted with the woman changing Branch's life, at least according to him.

Branch was puppydog eager but she didn't know how it was gonna go. What if she didn't like him? For sure he'd know it. She's always been an open book. A week could be a long time.

To her surprise, she liked Brendan from the first day they skied together. She hardly noticed his dents and scars; just those cabbage-ears from too much pounding. He was down to earth, sometimes funny, college-educated, courteous to her and soft-spoken. And his role as uncle when Branch was growing up counted for a lot. Branch had told her so much about those years.

They quickly discovered how well they were matched for exploring almost six thousand acres of slopes together. He was stronger but she was much more agile and experienced. Starting each day at the top of Lone Mountain, over two miles high, they raced each other laughing down four thousand vertical feet, startling dilettantes and debutantes decked out in the day-glo colors and miracle fabrics of the season. They skied every run they had time for, hitting diamond and double diamond bowls, chutes and terrain parks when they were feeling fresh, and then easing off to cruise intermediate slopes and take in spectacular views.

Then they'd pick up Branch, lodge-skiing and reading grow guides due to an injury building luxury homes here years back. If he was envious of the fun they were having, she couldn't see it. His delight in their taking to each other was obvious and unfeigned. They adjourned to drink and dine in sporty elegance on Brendan's platinum card. They'd try a new restaurant every night, barhop a little, eavesdrop on beautiful people who came this far to hang out with other beautiful people who came this far. From their booth the three of them would guess at professions based on attire and manner. Microsoft millionaire. Finance guy. Thousand a night callgirl. Coke dealer. Trophy wife.

Now, as the camera zooms in to show Brendan bounding up into the cage and jogging around, swinging his arms like an ape, pounding his chest, doing squats and jumps and mugging for the crowd, she's appalled. But Branch says, "He's looking real good. I think he might do okay."

"Bear's giving away a lot," Hampton says as fighter statistics are supered over their faces. "Age, for one. And he doesn't have that high-level grappling experience, all that BJJ."

Why do guys always have to act so knowledgeable? She'd bet money neither of them knows his ass from a hole in the ground about martial arts except what the announcers said two minutes ago. But no way is she going to ask what anything that starts with BJ stands for. With brothers you learn to head off wise-ass answers.

Branch helps her out. "Brazilian jiu-jitsu."

Watching drunks in the crowd cheer at nothing and flash gang signs at the camera, Laura hopes to live long enough to see most men cryogenically frozen and stuffed into giant space exploration vehicles to rocket off and colonize distant planets. Leave the rest of us here to recover this one we've been wrecking.

The fight starts and she hates it right off. This snarler's not the nice guy she knows.

She gets through the first round but only halfway through the second before the color guy shouts, "Look at that D'Arce choke. How beautiful is that?"

"Can't you turn that thing off?" she says. "How can you watch him get mauled this way?"

The guys ignore her, intent. Or think it's a rhetorical question, which it sure as hell is not. "At least turn down that damn screaming."

Laura reaches for the remote but Hampton blocks her with his caiman belly boots.

If this was a bar she'd snatch the device before Hampton knew what was going on. But not in his own house. Man's got his agenda and she's holding back until she knows what it is.

She's sure Hampton didn't invite her to come. Tough shit, Hampton. Get used to it. Branch includes her in just about everything that matters. Not courtesy or some togetherness thing. Except for a diminishing habit of stubbornness, he relies on her advice, the way she sees things, as he should. She slides closer on the pigskin couch and squeezes his leg before getting up and averting her eyes from the big-screen. She examines the bookcase, leatherbound first editions arranged by the color of their bindings.

Fight's over soon enough; at least there's that. Slantwise she glimpses scary damage before Branch takes the remote and says, "Which button I push?" Her cue to return to the couch for the next act.

Hampton breaks out brandy, a signal for the meeting to start. Fine with her. She declines a snifter, not ready to give up her bystander status just yet.

There's some introductory bullshit she ignores before Hampton tells Branch, "Since you're here, let's review the long-term plan. But now we've got this short-term problem to get out of the way first."

Branch says, "Which is?"

"Your partner there." A dismissive wave at the dark television screen. "No way he's transporting the load."

"Don't underestimate him," Branch says. "He's resilient. He'll heal up fast."

"Doesn't matter. Not looking the way he does. Cop spots those wounds, right away he thinks thug, figures some crime's involved. You know he'll search the car. Mule requirement number one is look clean-cut, aboveboard."

"Rather you not call Brendan a mule," Branch says. "He's just helping me out."

"How you look at it. But see it the way a cop does. Bust Bear for a felony amount, threaten him with years, find out where he got the stuff, which I don't much care about, and where it's going which I do. We got no choice, Branch. You're gonna have to go down and drive it up."

"Honey, no," Laura says. "Why you? Get somebody else. Or let Mr. Bigshot here do it, he wants it so bad."

"I'm distribution," Hampton says. "Branch is supply and I'm running out."

"I'm dry too," Branch says.

"So now you're a mule? When'd you sign up for that?"

"Darlin', we're talking about a special situation here."

"Got that right. Federal interstate felony's the technical term."

Hampton ignores her. "Your truck ready?"

"Always," Branch says.

"When can you leave?"

Laura pushes the anger out of her voice. "Honey, you see the way this escalates, how much trouble you could get in? Just grow for your patients."

"Can't produce enough. Not yet," Branch says.

"So back off. Drop some patients till you can."

"Look," Hampton says. She hears condescension drip. "You're just seeing one part, um, Laura. My dispensaries are falling all over themselves trying to be growers. It's way harder'n they think. The shelves are empty and they're chasing down street dealers, maybe a narc or two in there. Can't run a business that way. Branch has grow experience they don't. He'll solve the problem soon as I lock in a facility. Till then we do what we have to do. And that's him go south this time and bring back the weed."

"What's going on, Branch? That we haven't talked about."

"Mostly just growing a bit more than we planned 'cause we've found a better place. I was waiting to tell you till we made sure it's a go. Hamp's secured the location and he'll pay for everything. He's made me an offer to set it up and run it till his dispensaries get their act together. A real good offer. The pay's fine and I get to keep back enough medicine for my own patients. It's a real opportunity."

"Quantity?" Laura cuts to the chase. "More than ninety-nine plants? The federal limit?"

"Way more," Hampton says, pride in his voice. "They won't bother us. We're state-compliant, long as we've got the cards. Supply's got to match demand. Grow big or go home. Look at the bright side. After this run you won't have to worry about Branch or his uncle crossing state lines with California weed."

"It's only for a while," Branch says. "Once I save up enough to fund my own operation Hamp gets someone else to run his grow. There'll be plenty of takers."

"Seems like there's already one taker too many," Laura says. "We voted in the law we wanted, Branch. Stay inside it."

"Matter of funds," Branch says. "And timing."

"I'd say five or ten years in prison sure is a matter of timing. We've gone 'round and 'round about this."

"Have to look ahead," Hampton says. "What the legalities are going to be, not what they are now. Situation's way in flux. I'm looking for a lawyer to keep us all safe while we work on the legislature."

"Looking for? You send Branch across state lines while you look through the yellow pages? That's how you divide up responsibilities?"

"Brendan's never had no problems with the drive," Branch says.

"You're Brendan? You being in jail's the same as Brendan being in jail? Same to me? Same to us?"

Hampton says, "Calm down. We don't have to decide tonight. Let's give it a few days, see how quickly Bear recovers. Maybe you're right about his recuperative powers. If not, maybe we can put our patients off a few weeks, round up something local meantime."

Nobody who knows her ever tells her to calm down. "How about Branch just builds your setup. He consults. Find you somebody else once the plants are in the ground. Let them break the law, take the risk."

"Something to ponder," Hampton says. "But I thought he welcomed the chance. He who hesitates…"

Branch says, "It's big, Laura. Opportunity like this doesn't come along every day. This green rush won't last. We'll go world-class, put Montucky on the map."

"Montucky's already on the map. You ask Brendan's advice about this?"

"You know he'll insist on bringing it himself. Take the risk rather than me."

"Of course he will. And so he should, just like always. He's good at it and he likes to help out. Who're the two of you to be second-guessing him? Besides, he keeps talking about moving up here once he's done fighting. Isn't that what we just saw? Who'll notice a few extra bags if he's moving all his stuff, no matter how he looks?"

"Bear wants to come here?" Hampton says. "To live?" His eyes widen. "Girl, you just give me one hell of an idea. Tell you the truth, I'd rather've talked to Branch about this in private, let you guys hash it out after. But now? I'm glad you showed."

Branch says. "Darlin', you know I won't make this big a decision without you. We'll discuss it."

"Bet your ass we will."

"Whipped," Hampton mutters, too softly for most folks to notice. But growing up on a ranch your hearing gets real good. It's a survival skill. Calves bleating a mile away, wolves howling too close. Dogs by the hearth whimpering.

"Not whipped," Laura says right back. "Stroked. Smoothed out and coddled some. Pleasured." She doesn't put much into it, just enough to give Hampton a glimpse of what an unfettered Montucky woman might be like, even if she's not yet so good with the can apes.

Branch knows better than to say anything. He lets the conversation lapse into silence. Something she values in a man. Most don't know when to keep their damn mouths shut.

# CHAPTER THREE

# NOTHING XCEEDS LIKE XCESS

Brendan "Bear" Glass releases himself from the hospital against doctors' orders. Holes up for days before he's ready to confront his manager.

Natty Gason answers the knock at his ramshackle downtown San Jose apartment.

Brendan Glass clenches one big fist in Natty's Jesusfreak hair. The other bunches and twists the front of that stupid Mao jacket and lifts the skinny fart a foot off the floor. Slams him into the wall. "Cocksucker," Brendan says. "What the fuck did you give me?"

"Can't breathe," Natty says. "Put me down, I'll tell you."

"You tell me, we'll see if I put you down. Or out the window."

"Coumadin," Natty coughs. "Medication for heart patients."

"Hospital called it warfarin."

"Active ingredient."

"Looked it up. It's fucking rat poison. You gave me rat poison."

"Just some medicine in your energy drinks. Widely prescribed for hypertension. Thins the blood out some is all. Makes it easier to bleed."

"I'll say. But why? Why so much? I was spewing waterfalls. Couldn't see to defend myself. Got me all busted up, man."

Natty, still dangling, says, "How's I to know? Not like there's dosage information. Fans love a bloody fight and you sure gave 'em one. Nobody's thought of this before. We're blood brothers here on out. Dose it better next time. Put me down, you lug." He kicks Brendan in the nads.

Brendan gives him a ragdoll toss halfway across the living room.

Never know what to expect from the guy. Natty does a Chaplinesque goof on the whole thing. Dusts himself off like an old drunk thrown through swinging doors onto a dusty street. "Sit down'n I'll explain. We need to talk anyways before the conference call, get our story straight."

And like that it's over.

Natty leads Brendan past the usual cartons on the floor. Almost no furniture in the room, Natty not a guy to stay put for long. Same old coffee table and couch. But a few things catch Brendan's eye. Convenience store shelf displays line the coffee table, filled with thin packets of powder bearing a Crave logo. A 55-gallon drum with the lid off and a citrus smell in the air. A papercutter and a row of identical sealameal machines in the corner attached to a power strip.

Natty points to the couch. "Sit." As if he's in charge...

Brendan sits. Natty scrunches against the far end, sizing him up, wary.

"I'm the laughing stock of MMA," Brendan says. "You see the stories? New names I got? Crimson Mask? Red Badge of Courage? Ever find out what you give me, be calling me d-Con Jones."

"Won't. I hushed it up. Preached HIPAA to the doctors. Can't say a thing."

"Goddamn joke, me in a hospital. Massive transfusions, can't stop the bleeding? There goes my image. I'm a victim, first time in my life."

"Good thing you went, got those x-rays. Orbital fracture, you'd've shrugged it off, put ice on it. Blame the rest on me but I get a few points for that."

"Like hell. Account of you I couldn't see nothing but scarlet. Dude was hammering a blind man. You ruined my career, dumbfuck."

"Ruined? Gave it new life. Fight of the night, all that blood. Know how many calls I got since? Every manager with an up-and-comer making his cage debut wants you as his opponent. Know how many times that second round's been replayed? It's all over the Internet."

"Great. Just what I need, a new lowlight. Watch my ass get kicked a thousand times. Ain't words enough to describe the thrill."

"Means a bigger cut of a bigger purse next match-up," Natty says. "Problem is you're all hung up on your old image and it's been fading for years. Just one of many MMA fighters, hate to say it, past his prime. They all start to blur together. Time to decide what's your next role."

"Time for who to decide, me or you?"

"You, of course. But it's a manager's job, present you some alternative scenarios, get you back in the public eye. Got to be an archetype everyone can relate to. Battle-scarred veteran cop never says die. Old gunfighter faces down a trigger-happy new kid. Rocky whatever. But it's really got to be now. Twenty-first century take nobody's seen before. Less'n half-hour media bite to go viral."

"Present it to me? That's what you call it? Could've just said."

"Didn't know what would happen, Bear. Might've been nothing at all. Didn't see the need to upset you before the fight. Turned out epic, man. Maybe even iconic. Lots of ways we can go from here. Match you up with some young challenger you can kick the shit out of, be comeback story of the year."

"Ain't happening."

"You can milk your fame 'least a year longer in MMA, build up a little nest egg."

"Never going back in the cage, Natty. No mas nohow. What I came to tell you. I'll start coaching again if I have to."

"Well, what say we go the other way? You being a real TV star now with all that O.G. MMA pedigree in the background? You got fans, man. Let's work it. Let's work the hell out of it. I'll start pitching you for film roles. TV commercials, whatever. Yank the archetype right outside the cage. Can't you just see a Harley ad campaign? Could be the best thing ever happened to you. Keep you in the public eye for years. Look at the Rock. I'm your man for this, Bear. Make it happen for sure."

"Have at it," Brendan said. "Meanwhile, you mind, boss, I look into might some bigname training camp take me on? Work my way up, get me maybe my own gym someday?"

"That's what you wanna do, rest of your life? Jesus, Bear. No more'n that?"

"Don't see all that many options. Better'n skull fragments pokin' my brain. But I gotta say this, Natty. Not sure I still see a we in any of this. Not after what you done."

"Bullshit. Course there is. We made a lot of money together. Think I'm gonna abandon you now just 'cause your first career's in its twilight? You need a manager more'n ever, trust me."

"Trust the guy who poisoned me?"

"Maybe wasn't my best idea ever. But that was just the one."

"Wasting your breath, Natty."

"Not my only contingency plan, by the way. Just none as good as the blood thing. F'rinstance we better kick our network marketing up a notch while we figure out what else to do."

"How? Crave's not goin' anywhere."

"Not the way it is."

"Any truth to Vitasparc's gonna reformulate it?"

"Naw. I just invented that shit for a conference call one week all the news was bad."

"Might as well hang it up then. The rest of the Vitasparc line sucks worse."

"Right. Can't rely on them. Need a better product."

"Jump aboard some other pyramid scheme? Think we used that strategy up. Can't jerk our guys around again. They'll bail."

"As would I," says Natty. "Sick as anybody of that dance. Swap one miracle moneymaker for another? Start all over with new MLM projections sound just like the old ones? No way."

"So where's that leave us?"

"Create a new product of our own."

"Come on, Natty, get real. You know how much money it takes to bring one to market. How long it takes a new organization to build credibility."

"So we don't do that. We present a breathtaking improvement of an existing product we act as if comes from Vitasparc."

"I don't get it."

"Forget thinking outside the box. We think inside the drum." Natty walks him over to the big blue barrel. "Look like laundry detergent to you?"

"You say so."

"Customs gave me benefit of the doubt coming through Oakland but scared me half to death." Natty reaches past the convenience store displays to open an unmarked carton filled with empty packets the size of Chinese takeout soysauce. "Printed these up to look just like Crave packets 'cept for the name. This here's our new brand, you'n me."

Brendan reads the label:

*xCeed*
*because nothing xCeeds*
*like xCess*

"Plunk in our magic powder and we're good to go. Wanna guess how many packets that drum'll fill. How many thousands of dollars?"

Brendan says, "What happens when Vitasparc gets wind of us faking it's their product? You know they will."

"Maybe, but when? They're not watching us. Meanwhile we start piling up xCeed sales and street cred."

"Sooner or later, though..." Brendan says.

"Wouldn't do much at first. We're small potatoes. Maybe a cease and desist order. Put a hold on our commission checks? Threaten to kick us outta the family? Big whoop. We tell 'em right off we've already discontinued all sales. Then we kick Vitasparc to the curb. Put together our own marketing plan and a way better comp plan, bring all our guys over."

"Still might come after us. You hear about those guys 5-Hour Energy sued for counterfeiting years later? How much they had to settle for?"

"Yeah, but where'd be the evidence? Nobody hangs onto a used packet any more'n they would a used condom. Right off we burn all our existing packets and displays. Repackage the stuff in private-label ones we've been saving for an emergency. Design and words look nothing like Vitasparc or Crave so no infringement. We walk away clean, set up some LLC and get back to gettin.'"

"Suppose it ain't selling, just like it ain't selling now."

"Tell the organization adios. Buy back anything they're holding, fold up our tents and slip away."

Brendan says, "You know you're beating a dead horse, don't you? Don't shit a shitter. Way too many well-established energy drinks out there."

Natty digs his hands into the 55-gallon drum. Sifts powder through his fingers. "None like what you're looking at. Straight out of a secret spinoff lab back in Bangkok. Least that's the whisper story we tell our heavy hitters."

"Different how?"

"Secret ingredient? Fuck if I know. Yak sack, tiger jizz, ground up water buffalo package, rhino horn? They like all that shit over there. But tuk-tuk drivers been logging thirty-six hour shifts on it for years. There's no crime unless we false-advertise or it contains drugs. DEA won't pursue it and FDA won't have the time."

"So this stuff's legal?"

"Is over there. Believe me, you sell powder to millions of folks year after year in a death-penalty Golden Triangle place like Thailand, you know nothing criminal's in there. Our competitive advantage is so far it's strictly not for export."

"Except to you."

"'Cept to us, Bear. Told you, it's still me'n you. We spoon a few pennies' worth into xCeed packets, seal 'em up, stick 'em in Crave displays, get us a million percent markup or thereabouts, who's to know? And mark it up so our guys make out like bandits too."

Brendan shrugs at the barrel and says, "I guess you got enough for a market test. But what happens once it's gone?"

"We get us some more. Label a few drums over there on the manifest as fabric softener, a few as dish soap, whatever. But we gotta find one of them little international ports of entry boondoggled by some inland senator. One up in Montucky I want to look at since they mostly just export wheat. It's intermodal so it can go straight to train or truck."

"Still don't see it. Have to be crazy good."

"Let's us find out."

Natty gives him a long-handled spoon and shows him how much powder to put in a packet.

They position three filled packets side by side on sealameal machines. Natty presses down handles on two and Brendan the third, sucking out air and vacuum-sealing the xCeed pouches.

Natty uses a papercutter to trim the sealed tops evenly. He substitutes the xCeed packets in the front row of a Crave display and admires how perfectly they fit in the slots. "Never know, would you? Look real as can be. Fetch a couple of bottles of water from the fridge, would you?"

They drink enough to make some room in the bottles.

Natty snips open two packets and hands one to Brendan.

With thumb and forefinger they pooch the pouches open, pour the powder into the water bottles and screw the caps back on. They shake them up and hold them to the light, connoisseurs admiring the scary green color.

They uncap the bottles and inhale the bouquet.

"Chug-a-lug, chug-a-lug," Natty says.

Brendan says, "Makes you say hidey-ho."

They drain the bottles.

Brendan rocks a bit. "Burns your tummy, doncha know," he says. "Wow. Something's goin' on all right. What's the third batch for?"

From under his Jesus hair Natty gives him a big smile and a wink. He takes a cigarette paper out of the zigzag pack on the coffee table and crumbles in one of Johnny Legal's buds from the everpresent jar. He sprinkles the powder evenly on top and rolls a joint.

"The fuck you doing?"

"You're not in training now, man. Take a walk on the wild side."

Hands held up in mock horror, Brendan says. "I don't drink my pot. Don't smoke my energy drinks."

"Wuss." Natty shrugs. "More for me."

# CHAPTER FOUR

# HATTIE

Brendan's dad, Aloysius Glass, had been a third-generation Tightsqueeze underground copper miner. When the ten thousand miles of underground stopes and shafts played out, the Company moved most of their operations from Tightsqueeze to the Chucos country of Chile.

Rather than leave the little house in Dublin Gulch, Aloysius took a job at the Berkeley Mine though he despised open pit mining. Too many machines, too few men.

But when the Pit shut down the family had no choice. No more jobs. Hung on until Brendan finished the first grade before heading south. First into a rebuilt miner's cabin in Bisbee's Brewery Gulch. Then over to Globe before hopscotching the rest of Arizona, New Mexico and Utah. Finally Nevada, where Aloysius ran out of options, threw in the towel and died of black lung.

Changing small-town schools so often, Brendan found it hard to fit in until everyone discovered how good he was at sports. First Little League, then football and wrestling. Big for his age, strong and competitive, he was much in demand.

He liked living in Arizona best, mostly because it was a trainride away from his mom's family in Uvalde, Texas, where she'd been born. They were a wild and carefree bunch. Something was always going on and nobody minded the kids getting into mischief and raising hell. It was expected.

When Brendan Glass was thirteen, as soon as school was out he and his mom took the train over for a big gathering to celebrate one of his cousins getting married, something they did early and often.

But Hattie, his favorite, had made it to seventeen without getting hitched, even though she was, as she said, "real pretty and a whole lot of fun." The daughter of his mom's oldest sister, Hattie had always liked Brendan as much as he liked her. They had good times together and there was always a dare to it.

The morning after they arrived, Hattie grabbed a .22 and a box of bullets after breakfast without asking and told everybody she was taking Brendan to the ranch to gun down some jackrabbits. She slapped the shells in his hand, said, "Make yourself useful," and led him out to her old blue pickup.

As soon as she turned off the highway onto the farm-to-market road, Brendan knew which ranch she meant. It was a couple of hundred acres of land too poor for cattle, supporting sheep only if you used a pear burner to singe spines off the prickly pear cactus. Even then it took ten acres a head if the sheep were hardy, like the Navajo Churros her uncle ran.

No real house on the place, just a few outbuildings. She pulled past a lambing shed to some rough living quarters, rolled down her window and shouted, "Anybody home?"

After a few moments of silence she leaned on the horn.

"Expecting someone?" Brendan said.

"No, just making sure we're alone," Hattie said. "Normally wets only stay here when we're shearing or lambing. You want to walk a bit or just shoot from the cab?"

"Let's walk before it gets any hotter," Brendan said.

After a few minutes he handed her the rifle so he could take off his shirt to tie around his waist.

"You're filling out real good," Hattie said. "Be a handsome man in a year or so. Fact is, I didn't know better, I'd say you're old enough now to do, you know, man things."

"Like what?"

She handed him back the rifle and grinned. Unbuttoned one button of her red checkered shirt and then another. "Too bad girls can't do what boys do."

"Girls do whatever they want," Brendan said. "Least around here."

"Think so? Out here in front of God and everybody?"

"I don't see no everybodies."

"You want to see mine?"

"Hell yeah." Not thinking she'd do it.

Hattie whipped off her shirt and moved up on him. He stepped back.

"Relax," she said. "I don't bite. I just want to tie this where you tied yours."

Brendan stood stock-still as she reached around him and tied her shirt to his waist and then stepped back.

They stood there for a few moments before she busted out laughing.

"What's so funny?"

"You are," she said. "Trying so hard not to look. It's okay if you do. Fact I'll be pissed if you don't, I go to all this trouble. Some guys, opportunity like this'd be pretty bold to tell me how fine they are."

Fine wasn't the half of it. Her breasts were perfect and he was sure she knew it. Not that he'd seen any up close like this in the flesh, but she looked every bit as good as the girls in the magazines under his bed.

"What say you rest the rifle up against that mesquite?" she said. "So's it won't get a mind of its own and go off."

He did but then didn't want to look straight at her, still shy.

"We make a nice looking pair," Hattie said.

Brendan got up his nerve. "You make a nice looking pair all by yourself."

"Now you're talking." She drew near. "You want to bump titties?"

He felt his face go red.

She reached around and grabbed his butt, leaned back and started bouncing her chest off his.

It didn't take long before his erection pressed against her. He tried to tilt his chest forward and his ass back.

Hattie stuck her hands in his hip pockets and held herself against him. "Don't be silly. I'm right proud you like me."

Brendan was in no-man's land. No idea what to do with his hands as she stood jammed up against him, rubbing her breasts back and forth, up and down. Her hips too. He was dumbstruck.

She loosened his belt and unbuttoned his jeans. He started to tremble in the heat.

She unbuttoned his fly and he started to stammer out something that didn't seem to have words.

"Hush up," she said. "Let mommy."

His jeans fell to his knees and then to his feet.

She grasped him, dropped to her knees and began rubbing his dick against her stiff nipples, back and forth.

Nothing ever felt like that. Nothing could be so smooth and soft and silky. Except maybe...

She positioned him dead center and pressed her breasts to each side, tunneling him. Rocked back and forth once or twice and that was that. He came prodigiously.

She rubbed his spurting cock over each breast in turn.

Dizzy, he almost blacked out for a moment.

She rose to her feet, dragged an index finger over some of his jism and stuck it in her mouth. Slurped it noisily. "Ever taste your ownself?"

"Whaddaya mean?"

"What do I mean, Brendeen? Lick me clean, Brendeen. Lick me clean."

She advanced on him and he almost bolted. This was all happening too fast.

"What're you worried about? Might get an appetite for it? Tasting spuzz'll turn you queer? It's yours, not somebody else's. Get to know thyself."

He couldn't speak.

She scooped up more, pointed it at his mouth like a gun and charged him.

He ran. Sad to say, but he ran.

She chased him, laughing, until finally he was laughing too.

She cantered over to an old-fashioned pump handle, dropped her jeans—no undies—and bellied up to it. She lowered herself and rubbed against the up-poised metal, back and forth, until she chirped and sighed, feigning an orgasm. Or maybe, for all he knew, not.

"Thank God we got that out of the way," she said. "Best of all, neither you nor me got the least bit pregnant. Now we can relax and have us some fun. Clean yourself off so they don't pick up our scent when we get back."

Brendan felt suddenly shy. He didn't want Hattie watching him wash and dry his penis, give it too much attention or not enough.

"Oh for God's sake," she said. She exercised the pump handle, in the normal way this time, and splashed water all over herself, rubbing deeply where it mattered. When she was done she stood silently for a moment regarding him. And he her. This vision right now, he knew, water beading her pelt and her breasts, her face and her hair, droplets gleaming in the west Texas sun, would live in him to his dying day.

Hattie grabbed her shirt but didn't put it on. She got in the truck and made a big deal out of whistling a popular Hank Snow tune while looking away as he squirted himself down and rinsed himself off.

As he pulled on his pants she sang a few lines about no more walking the floor with a burning inside. "We call that the Vaseline song," she said.

Which was way more words than was in him to offer back as they drove around and shot jackrabbits, startling him the way they jumped straight up in the air and squeaked or squealed or made this tiny little scream before they thumped down dead.

Hattie let him drive around the ranch a bit before she took the wheel. As if he needed something else new to think about. His first sexual encounter, first time he drove, first time he killed something. Jesus. All on the same day. Last Friday he was taking his algebra final. He had an Asshole in Wonderland feeling.

Once he and his mom returned to Arizona he kept reliving that day. Wondered when would he see Hattie again. Could he grow up fast enough to... To do what? Be her man?

Come fall, though, he heard Hattie'd got herself married. Lucky guy, whoever he was.

Next thing he got word of was they'd been bit by the religion bug and joined up with some church outfit between Dallas and Austin. Moved there and all.

# CHAPTER FIVE

# CROPTOBER

It's coming up on hunting season in the sere hills and evergreen woodlands of California's emerald triangle. Up here they call it Croptober.

Harvests in ahead of the hunters, CAMP surveillance helicopters come and gone, itinerant trimmers thumbing their way back to wherever they came from, it's buyer time.

In one of Mendocino's larger towns not far from the freeway, a chocolate-covered crewcab pickup sporting Montucky plates and diamondplate crossbed and sidemount toolboxes pulls into the driveway of a nicely tended but anonymous older two-story residence.

A motion detector above the entryway alerts a closed-circuit camera as the driver climbs the porchsteps.

Before Branch can ring the bell Brendan Glass opens the stash house door and greets him with the usual bearhug. "C'mon in, man. Glad you made it down okay. Been a while."

Branch Howell, dressed cowboy, steps into an art deco living room where two men are settled into an overstuffed velvet couch. One looks like a big aging hippie or surfer; the little guy some odd kind of mystic.

Brendan introduces them with an armsweep. "This is Johnny Legal, my lawyer. Keeps medical marijuana on the up and up. This over here is Natty, my manager. Asked him to sit in." The mystic.

To them, "This here's my nephew Branch D. He's Montucky through and through but stems from the wacko Texas side of the family—"

Branch gives Brendan a hard stare. "Don't you go there," he says.

Johnny "Legal" Siegel rises, extends his hand for a shake. "No plans to. Not my kind of place."

Wasn't what Branch meant or who he was talking to, but he's glad to let it slide.

Natty gives him a too-cool-to-get-up wave.

Branch says, "Didn't expect a crowd. Rather do my—"

"Relax," Brendan says. "They're just here for when your friend comes to make his pitch. Follow me."

On the stairs Branch says, "Hope I wasn't out of line. Don't care for witnesses. You said lawyer, kind of set me off."

"No problem," Brendan says. "Everything's cool."

Upstairs the parlor looks and smells like a rich coffee emporium.

Brendan guides Branch to an aubergine Victorian sofa. On a marble coffee table, half a dozen one-pound paper sacks are flanked by five-pound foil bags of exotic fair-trade coffees and loose organic teas.

"Appears somebody's gone into the coffee business," Branch says.

"That would be you. Story you tell, you get pulled over, you're down here doing your research on roasteries, taking back samples before you open up a coffeehouse. It's sealed up tight and we took a few other precautions, but I don't know there's any way to mask a smell from a trained K9. They pick up on lots of different smells at once. But you ain't likely to run into one of those, you stay on the freeways, and it'll get by most people if they don't have reason to be suspicious."

"So what's what?" Branch says.

"The OG Kush is in the big coffee bags. Neville's Haze is inside the tea. They ask you to open something, do the small sacks. Anything says Graffeo is just coffee. Tell 'em the others are all vacuum-packed. Busting 'em open will ruin the freshness, make 'em unsalable. Which, if you think about it, sure as hell will."

"Appreciate the stealth," Branch says. "But who's paying for all of this? I only brought enough cash—"

"All part of the service," Brendan says. "Somebody we know has a chain of hip tea and artisanal coffee shops. Cop sees these varieties he's never heard of he'll believe your story, you tell it well."

"'Preciate the cover, Brendan. Laura'll be relieved. She worries."

"Didn't think I was doing it for you, did you? How is that fine young woman?"

"Doing great. Sailin' toward another degree."

"'Bout the money, though," Brendan says. "We came up a half-pound short on the Kush; big run on it last week 'cause it's real good. So you can hang onto some of your money or I can give you"—gesturing toward the big burlap coffee sack in the corner—"this in trade."

Branch walks over and hefts the sack. "Damn. How much is in here?"

"Couldn't say. All we got. Never weighed it out. Totes like a big bag of dog food so maybe twenty pounds, maybe more. It's a closeout special called Harlequin, supposed to be high CBD and low THC. Good rep for pain relief but seems like it wasn't meant to be. They were clones but some must've hermied out, grew some bananas. It was kind of an aeronautical emergency so they got pulled and rough-trimmed in a hurry. It's mostly bud but there's some seeds here and there. If you can use it, sell it for next to nothing and you still come out ahead. If not, we'll deduct the price the next time around."

"Not sure there'll be a next time, Brendan. Hope to have a rotating harvest up and running, time this is gone."

"More power to you, man. Get us past this short-term foolishness. Thing to consider, though, is we haven't had time to seal this up so we'll just have to stick it inside a bunch of garbage bags. Don't know if you want to take the risk."

Branch sniffs around the bag and says, "It ain't that bad. I think I can squeeze it into my crossover toolbox. It's pretty heavy watertight aluminum and I added some closed-cell foam around the gasketing before I left. I'll cover the bag up with tools and just not pull over long enough for anyone to notice. Once I get up in the mountains it'll be cool enough the smell won't carry much."

Brendan says, "We sewed the bag shut but I can snip open a few stitches if you want to take a look at it before you decide."

"Naw," Branch says. "I trust you, man. And I got a pretty big financial incentive until I can bring in a crop. This'll help."

Brendan reaches into the coffee table drawer and pulls out a pair of vacuum-sealed quarter-ounce packets and a pair of scissors. "Couple of samples. This one's the Haze. And this here's the OG."

Brendan cuts open both bags and hands them to Branch, who dumps out some buds, holds them to his nose, squeezes them gently, inhales deeply.

Brendan says, "Smaller buds, most of 'em, than what we sell to the bag-appeal dispensaries. But it's all good."

"You've come through again," Branch says. "Much obliged." He hands over a fat envelope. "Want to count it?"

"Nope. Want to twist one up for the road?"

"Naw, I'll wait till I'm back home. Better safe'n sorry."

"Up to you," Brendan says.

"Lemme use your phone."

"What, don't have yours?"

"Battery's in my other pocket. Far as I'm concerned, GPS stands for Government Peeping Secretly. Nobody but Laura and Hampton knows I'm down here and I'm keeping it that way."

Branch dials Hampton's cell from memory while Brendan says, "I'll vouch for both strains, the way they work. The Haze is my preference. Been a guinea pig for pain relief these last few weeks."

"I can tell," Branch says. "Never seen you so bruised up." He lifts his hand as Brendan starts to reply. He says into the phone, "We're ready for you now," and hangs up. "What do the doctors say?"

"Shattered eye socket's the worst of it. One more operation, try to fuse my orbital rim. Be on the road to recovery then. Slow, though."

"Fight was real hard to watch. Laura couldn't."

"I didn't see much of it either. You hang onto that woman whatever you do."

"Trying. You're moving kind of careful too."

"Broke a couple of ribs. One pokes at my spleen when I cough. That'll heal, I suppose. Or not. It's the eyebone ends my career. Can't take another hit up there. Too close to where I live. And you know everybody'd be aiming for it. Might as well paint a target around it, look like Spuds MacKenzie. Time to move on. Maybe swing back up your way, depending on what your buddy's got in mind."

"Always room for you at the ranch. Shitfire, we'd love to get you back to Montucky for good, Brendan."

"See what happens. Howzabout you pull your rig into the garage away from prying eyes. There's plenty of trash bags waiting." Brendan gathers sacks of coffee. "I'll help you load through the kitchen."

Once the truck's toolboxes are full and locked, Brendan leads Branch into the living room from the attached garage and gives Johnny Legal the all-clear nod.

After a few minutes of small talk, Hampton arrives to be introduced. He's dressed and groomed like the western real-estate guy he is.

Branch tells Brendan, "Hamp's our business brains. I'd like him to take you through what we have in mind, see if you're interested."

"The Bear's dance card is pretty full," Natty says. His black outfit on closer examination, Branch decides, is more monk than punk.

"Still," says Hampton.

Johnny Legal says, "Can't hurt to listen. Be an education anyway. All I know about Montucky is grizzlies'n skinhead militias. Whatever a Unabomber is. Sounds like a kid's toy."

Hampton says, "Don't believe all you read. We've got some real advantages. A mighty skimpy medical marijuana law for one. Till the legislature meets again in two years we're wide open. Not at all like here. Law says one-to-one relationship, caregiver-to-patient, six plants for every patient you sign. Once a patient's yours nobody else can sell to him, long as you keep him satisfied. No limit how many you can supply."

"Long as you got somebody supplying you," says Johnny Legal. "Why your boy's here again."

Hampton nods. "You're right. Expertise is our big challenge. But the opportunity is way bigger. What I do's buy and manage properties, and I got hit real hard because of the economy. Medical cannabis is starting to change that. I'm converting buildings to dispensaries across the state and staffing 'em with caregivers as best I can."

Johnny says, "Caregivers are easy. Dispensaries are easy. Good growers, not so much. The kind of growers you need are thin on the ground."

"We're finding that too, but it's early yet. Branch is starting to get some good results. Plan is for him to ramp up with a big operation until everybody gets the hang of it."

Johnny says, "Not doubting you or his ability, but this isn't the first time we've provisioned him up. What's taking you?"

Hampton says, "Mostly just enough square footage and infrastructure. Got a building under contract now that's perfect and I've got the buildout money standing by."

"Large commercial grows are harder to set up and run than you might think," Johnny says.

"Even harder to conceal," Natty says.

"That's where Brendan comes in," says Branch.

"Not much the farmer type," says Johnny Legal.

"'Xactly," Branch says. "What better front than a gym? Equipment coming in. People going out with big gym bags. Who's to notice what's growing in the top floors?"

Hampton says, "A martial arts academy makes business sense anyway. I'd do it even without a grow operation, get a name like Bear to run it. Tightsqueeze is a mile high. Already has a winter Olympic sports training facility edge of town, bobsledding and skiing, biathlons, all that. They do okay even though nobody really gives a shit about Winter Olympics most of the year. Meanwhile MMA's growing fast and it kind of fits in with our rough and tumble. Be ten times the interest, we had a Bear Glass high-altitude training camp."

Brendan says, "Everybody trains at altitude now if they're scheduled to fight in thin air like Denver or Mexico City. Otherwise you run out of gas. I use Albuquerque; most big names do. Or Boulder or Easton. But they're real pricey."

Hampton says, "I can set you up in a great old building for nothing, all the room you can ever use. It'll outclass any converted warehouse you see on television. Town's loaded with cheap living quarters and restaurants and bars for fighters and trainers. Elegant old restored hotel for visiting journalists and TV crews. Be like a poor man's destination resort."

Brendan says, "Tightsqueeze, America. I like Tightsqueeze. All the room in the world for outdoor cardio. Run right up to the Continental Divide and down again in time for lunch."

Hampton says, "Building was designed back in the day by a well-known architect. Was a boomtown YMCA in the Twenties. Big elegant main rooms. Full basketball court with a running track above. Lap pool, steam room just needs a refurbish. I buy and provide the building, no cost to you. Everything you need to set up is on me, first year at least. Run it your way. Bring your promoter here to manage the gym too, do the marketing, advertising, publicity, whatever. Year one I'll bankroll that as well."

Natty says, "Sounds like a plan. But I'm a city guy. Not sure I'd fit in there. Or want to."

Hampton says, "Never know. You might like it more'n you think. Huge potential. It's not about one town or one gym or one year. It's about the whole damn state, years to come. I want to own the market. Nobody's thinking big as me. Nobody leans in the way I do. So far nobody else with the money to move on the opportunity is that interested yet.

Johnny leans forward, interested. "How much money you figure you'll need?"

"To build out the facility? Million might do it. Maybe a million two. I got a hard stop right about there until it produces. Meanwhile I already got enough buildings for dispensaries scattered around the state to attract limited partners and investors. As long as nobody knows where the product is coming from at first, the outlets will pretty much take care of themselves. Time's the bigger issue. It's all about staking the claims first and building the clientele."

Johnny says, "I guess it's up to you, Brendan. Legally I don't think you've got much risk. You'd be just a tenant."

Hampton says, "You're key, Bear. I need a legit, visible enterprise on the main floors or I can't afford all the infrastructure buildout or easily hide all the comings and goings. So if you're interested, Bear, just figure out what you need to make it work. Johnny, same goes for you. I could sure use help with the legalities. Position us for the future. There's loopholes I know a savvy attorney could have fun with."

Natty says, "You couldn't do better. Johnny here's the behind-the-scenes guy put together the Mendocino zip-tie program, fifty bucks a plant for regular sheriff inspections and protection."

Hampton says, "That was you?"

A modest Johnny nod.

Hampton says to Johnny, "You got any interest at all, I'll fly you up, put you up, give you the full tour."

"Brendan, it's a natural," Branch says. "Town's always been famous for its barfights. Your reputation'll bring 'em in from all over."

Brendan says to Hampton, "Your footing the bill include some sort of salary for me till I'm up and running? I gotta have something to live on."

"Expense it. Expense it all. Natty too, if you both come on board. I'll fund a joint account. Proceeds first year all go to you. Rather not be an employer. Arm's length is better. Maybe a draw against what you take in. You come up short some month, I make up the difference. We'll work it out."

Natty says, "Problem I see's the recommend. Still need that, don't you? Many doctors up there ready to write one, be known as a pot doctor?"

"You put your finger on it," Hampton says, "way things are now. But we'll get there. Good money, some guy fresh out of med school, pay off those student loans. Or an oldtimer ready to cut down his practice. Hundred fifty to say go do it. Don't take that long to say."

"How much of that the doctors get to keep?"

"All so far."

"Seems like an opportunity," Natty says. "Maybe I get me a white robe and a stethoscope, forge a medical diploma from the Dominican Republic or somewhere."

"Might not have to go to those lengths. I can see you having a big role with the gym from day one. Building's ready for a big exhibition ring, cage, whatever you call it. Put on events. Sound system, good seating, video cameras if you need them."

Natty says, "Hard to believe you got more opportunity than Cali." He looks over at Johnny Legal and Brendan. "But we'll talk it over 'mongst ourselves. We're interested, we'll get back to you."

"Work it through Branch if you do," Hampton says. "Anybody benefits, he should too."

Branch says, "Another thing. Wonder if we can make some kind of side deal, get the benefit of your genetics. Plenty of expertise we don't have yet back home. Frankly, not many people up there I can ask and YouTube and weed forums help but not enough."

"Don't know the half of it," Johnny says. "Speaking of which, Brendan, he take that big bag?"

"Loaded up."

Branch nods. "My girlfriend'll love me bringing her some seeds."

"Maybe if I come up there she'll love me a little bit too," says Johnny Legal.

Branch starts to come up out of his chair.

# CHAPTER SIX

# PLUNDER

Old Hugh Glass bolted from his Fort Kiowa newspaper reporter interview, sick of people after only an hour among 'em. He loped across the plains, away from the keelboat anchored in the Missouri shallows. Out of habit he settled into a long groundeating stride, his gait uneven because of the badly healed leg snapped like a twig—a sound he still heard—by the first mighty swipe of the grizzly paw that he now wore as a necklace tied around his neck by its sinews.

For an hour he crossed dips and dry rills, tall desiccated grasses the color of his deerskin leggings crackling under his moccasins. He topped a slight eminence that provided a view for miles around, hoping to spot bison in the distance or antelope up close. Find 'em now and track 'em in the morning.

Nothing to be seen so he hunkered down in a comfortable squat, his mind on the past. He regretted that damnfool story he'd made up years ago about the Pawnees, never dreaming it'd go as far as it did or be read by people he'd never met.

Truth was, First Mate Glass and his captain, Jimmy Forrest, had enjoyed the pirate life up to the very last minute when a Lafitte corsair boarded an American merchant vessel and scuttled it at Matagorda, bringing down the wrath of the navy. The *Enterprise*, a swift American man-of-war, sailed unobstructed toward Galveston Bay with instructions to destroy all of Campeche if the buccaneer didn't surrender the island.

Lafitte ordered his men to set fire to La Maison Rouge and the fort before scattering their ships to all points of the compass, leaving the man-of-war nothing to shoot at or sink. He asked for a few brave volunteers to remain and bury the bulkier and heavier booty while he escaped on his fastest brig, the *Pride*, with all the silver, jewels and gold it could carry.

Glass and Forrest were quick to volunteer. The last to leave harbor, they almost took a hit from a cannonball close enough to splash the deck of their small cutter. But Forrest was a fearless and adroit skipper. Once the American navy had surveyed the razed little town and returned to the Enterprise to lie up in harbor for the night, the two shipmates sailed back undetected through the twilight to the lee side of the island. Working all night, they unburied the plunder and lightered it out to their small ship.

Plunder. Hugh Glass's favorite word then and now. You could plunder something. You could plunder somebody, the way they did the old pirate who'd been plundering for years. The plunder was yours if you could hang onto it and keep your mouth shut. Or hide it until the coast was clear.

They sailed east through the Gulf of Mexico heavy with loot, staying close to shore through the night and lying low each day in some smuggler's cove, inlet or bayou where there was plenty of time to plan. Could they stay undetected the whole trip so no word of them would get back to Lafitte once his men returned to the island to find only empty holes? Where could they cache the treasure?

They decided to split up and rendezvous in six years to uncache the plunder. Forrest would take the empty ship to New Orleans, sell it, and retire to live off the proceeds, giving them a cover story. Hugh Glass would go overland where no one would recognize him. He planned to travel light until he reached St. Louis, where he could head upriver. The only treasure on his mind now was beaver pelts, anonymous and easy to carry. Nobody there for him to plunder but the beaver, and them unable to defend or retaliate. Nobody there to plunder him, or so he'd thought…

Hugh Glass rose from his squat on the hillock, favoring the bum leg that cramped up on him if he didn't stay moving.

# CHAPTER SEVEN

# PARADISE VALLEY

Almost eight years to the day after hearing that Hattie got married, just as Brendan Glass was graduating from college, he got his first and only letter from her. She all but begged for his help with her young son, Branch.

It'd been too painful to remain in Texas after the fire that killed the boy's father, so she'd changed their names at the courthouse and moved up to Montucky. The Church Universal and Triumphant had bought a 12,000 acre Paradise Valley spread on the banks of the Yellowstone.

She went on about the church's charismatic leader, Elizabeth Clare Prophet—Guru Ma—reincarnated as Messenger of the Ascended Masters. She tried to explain something Brendan didn't get about a violet flame and the power of non-stop highspeed chanting she called decreeing.

Uh-oh. Sounded like whatever religious bug bit her back in Texas still had a hold on her.

It's beautiful here, the letter continued, but so cold and windy in the winter. Sometimes hard to keep the faith alive, not to mention young children and the elderly in families where wage-earners had to go elsewhere for work.

Many had maxed out credit cards, stockpiling provisions and building shelters, sure there would be no banks or credit card companies left standing by the next billing cycle. When the day came that El Morya had prophesied Russian nuclear attack ushering in the apocalypse, the whole community huddled in huge bomb shelters where they chanted, armed to the teeth, ready to repel anyone who tried to get in.

After a couple of days they declared victory, saying such powerful decreeing had prevented the bombing. The credit card statements arrived in a couple of weeks.

Folks in town who'd given them the benefit of the doubt hated and feared them now. They said the weapons weren't for the Russians but to gun down any neighbors seeking food, medical help or protection from radiation. Harder now to stay on the spiritual plane pushing a shopping cart past whispers of heathen deathcult brainwashing.

What had Hattie gotten herself mixed up in this time? Who were these people? Brendan had never heard of them. And the boy? Hadn't he been through enough?

He hit the college library first thing in the morning. Found newspaper accounts of tens of millions of dollars constructing an underground bunker complex. Federal charges of illegally obtaining armed personnel carriers, paramilitary supplies, and heavy-duty assault weapons including 120,000 rounds of tracer and 6-inch armor-piercing incendiary ammunition for their nine .50-caliber semiautomatic Barrett M82s.

Brendan did the math. Over 13,000 rounds per rifle. That's not just plinking. He didn't know what twelve thousand acres looked like, but he bet nine M82s with a range of over a mile, properly positioned, could easily defend the inhabited part.

The incendiary Raufoss Mk 211 armor-piercing rounds were world-class issue for snipers too. A projectile that large was overkill for taking out a rancher at a time. But pivoting the Barrett on its bipod from hard target to soft without reloading was a big advantage.

International conventions generally prohibited using this weapon and ammunition for anti-personnel purposes. But the U.S. hadn't signed on and, besides, this wasn't really warfare.

People in favor said it wasn't inhumane because the round exits the body before the firebomb explodes. But it was ideal for targets wearing body shields. No ballistic vest can stop a penetrator designed for helicopters and tanks, but the shield would slow the projectile enough for the incendiary flash to kick off inside the body, flash-broasting flesh from the inside out.

Armed, if that was the word, with this information, Brendan went home and reread the last part of Hattie's letter. Despite the difficulties, she wasn't worried about herself. But her boy Branch was withdrawn and moody, traumatized by what had happened to his dad. The church's belief in karmic ascension, shedding one bodily embodiment to assume the next, wasn't helping the way she'd hoped. He needed a man's influence he could trust. Any chance Brendan might come up for a few weeks and try to bring Branch out of his shell?

The timing couldn't be better. With no career plans, Brendan had accepted a job offer to coach wrestling at a New Mexico junior college come fall. He was free to head up to Montucky for the summer and see what Hattie was like now.

She didn't sound much like the fun-loving woman he still dreamed about. She made it clear he wouldn't be coming as a boyfriend. He had no problem with that. The lad deserved a break. And who better than a close relative who'd first enjoyed the same breasts? Spend some time on the river, hike the park, climb a few mountains, get the boy away from the wackos. Maybe find ranch work bucking bales to pay for the summer and stay in shape.

He wrote Hattie a brief note saying he was on his way, piled camping gear into his beater station wagon and made his slow way north, exploring back roads through country he'd never seen that resonated inside him like distant memories.

The church the locals called CUT was weird enough, but Branch seemed none the worse for it. He welcomed his uncle without ceremony and they eased into an undemanding friendship.

The boy was only seven but already pretty athletic and used to going wherever he wanted. He loved the outdoors and showed Brendan places along the Yellowstone where he'd been taking solitary walks.

When Brendan inflated his raft, Branch just smiled, which was about as expressive as he ever got. They called themselves the river rats. Planned excursions as if they were the first *voyageurs* to ever explore the Yellowstone. Or they'd just wander around the ranch and surrounding hills. If Branch tired, Brendan hoisted him onto his shoulders like a piece of exercise equipment and started jogging, the boy banding his hands around Brendan's forehead to hang on.

Church members showed little interest in the natural world they called the physical plane. To Brendan they seemed to be from everywhere in the world except where they were. They worked outside, or tried to, but seemed more comfortable inside a building or tent, talking and talking and talking or chanting and singing.

Young Branch was already carrying tools and light materials to help CUT construction teams build shelters for the believers they called *chelas*. The ragged assortment of trailers they'd moved up from the old California headquarters offered scant winter protection.

Hattie had everybody's respect and fit easily into their community. But to Brendan she seemed tired and worn down. Overserious. He missed the old spark and the banter.

After a few evenings sleeping on her couch, he pitched a tent by the river a quarter-mile away. After dawn exercises he'd come to their little house for breakfast and then take the boy out for the day.

As August waned, he started packing his gear. Branch watched with a wary animal look but neither of them said anything until their last raft trip of the season. The Yellowstone was low and clear now and they drifted slowly downstream. They watched ducks and geese heading south along the flyway. Brendan unshipped oars and said, "You know I'm going to do that too."

"Why?" Branch said.

"I have a job. Just like you have to go back to school. I'm a teacher."

"You're a good one."

"So are you, Branch. You showed me a lot. Thanks for that. And for making me feel at home here with you and your mom."

"But you're not coming back," the boy said.

"Why not? Teachers don't work in the summer."

"Is it cold where you teach? Can I come visit you in the winter?"

Brendan said, "Let's wait until you're a little older. Then we'll ask her."

# CHAPTER EIGHT

# BULL WHAT

Laura Engebretson pushes aside the final draft of her Animal Science master's dissertation. Snow's sheeting outside her window. First real weather of the season with an advisory calling for seventy-five mile per hour gusts but it looks more like maybe fifty now as the storm passes through. She's watching bent-over trees sway like elegant dancers in a misty twilight Chinese painting, waiting for Branch to call.

Before he left he said he wouldn't be phoning from the road. Call it a security measure, call it cautious, call it paranoid, it's classic Branch.

She's not the worrying sort but can't help it now. What if he gets this close and spins out or somebody runs him off the road and into a barrow pit. Highway Patrol comes, searches, it's all over.

Think of something else. Get back to her blog.

One June night in a saloon Einar Engebretson met Nelson Story, a man his own age, twenty-five. Little guy but seething with energy and ambition. A freight driver from Denver, Story had just come up over the Bozeman Trail, only recently widened for wagons. He told Einar his plan: peddle the provisions and then sell off the wagons, ox teams and pack mules. Pan for gold until it got too cold and then head back south to do it all over again next spring.

Engebretson said, "How 'bout I look at what you've got first thing in the morning?"

"I just sell to merchants," Story said. "I'm not a drummer has time to go around to everybody. Got to find some of that gold."

Engebretson said, "Give me first look. I'll outbuy any merchant here. Stores are hurting. Lots of miners pulling out, heading over to Alder Gulch. Rumor is they struck it big."

"Ready for another whiskey?" Story said. "Alder Gulch? Where's that at?"

"Straight east along Grasshopper Creek gets you to the Beaverhead. Ruby Valley's on the other side."

"Think a mule'd make it across this time of year?"

Engebretson said. "Not likely. Someone'll pole you across. Got a big raft."

"My camp's a couple of miles west of town. Come out first light. Bring your gold."

No problem finding Story's camp at dawn. Einar heard and smelled the animals before he saw them. All he had with him was his doeskin poke, his balance scale and its weights.

"Ready to do business?" Story said first thing.

Engebretson held out the pouch.

"Lemme see," Story said. "Don't rightly know what it looks like and I come all this way."

Einar untied the rawhide drawstring, pinching out a few nuggets and some dust into the palm of the hand he extended to the teamster.

"Damn if it ain't pretty enough," Story said. "Just waiting to be found, eh?"

"Was while it lasted. Be early to the next place, will be there."

"Tell me what you need. I show you what I got."

"How 'bout t'other way around? We need everything."

They walked past each wagon, Einar pointing out items he wanted. One of Story's bullwhackers unloaded them. Another carried them over to an oxcart while a wrangler started harnessing two oxen to it and hitching a packmule behind.

Once done, the wagon was full of tools and implements, cook gear and blankets and goods enough to provision the new farm community.

Story toted up the cost.

Engebretson didn't dicker. He showed Story how to use weights on one side of the balance beam and gold on the other. "Bigger scales in the stores. Get someone to weigh out what I give you and tell you what it's worth. You'll see I'm fair. Don't let 'em trade you for greenbacks or Seated Liberties, much less Confederate greybacks. No way to know what any of 'em'll be worth once the war's over. Everybody takes gold."

"Best get me mine then."

Engebretson finished weighing out. "You got something to put this in?" he said, handing over some nuggets. "When your wagons are empty I'll buy them too, the oxen and the mules if the price is right."

"If everybody's leaving how come you're buying so much."

"I got my gold already—enough to ranch and farm in a big way. Family's here to help. Some of the best topsoil and prettiest grazing land just up in those foothills. Ride up there with me, you'll see. Then you can bring back your cart and oxen till you don't need them anymore."

Story detached a big tradesman's wallet from his belt, folded the gold into a large greenback and thrust it down into a flapped compartment.

"You better get you a poke," Engebretson said.

"Been thinking about just that. Know where?"

"Mercantile's got 'em."

"No, you know, get me a poke."

Einar wasn't a prude but he was a family man now and a Norwegian to boot. "Try the saloons. Not the one we was in last night but the others. Ain't but a few of them ladies around. You'll know 'em when you see 'em. They look real tired and muddy from miners crawling all up and down 'em."

They climbed onto the oxcart, sat side by side buckboard style, and slowly made their way north toward the Pioneers.

Within an hour they started passing new homesteads filled with activity. Men, women, and a surprising number of kids of all ages were tending row crops and building houses.

"Damn," Story said. "You got you a real settlement going."

"Working on it," Engebretson said with satisfaction. "We know how. Have 'er in good shape come winter. This is my place here."

"Damn. Look at that pasture. Look at that grass."

Engebretson was proud of the way the dew glistened in the morning sunlight. "Look better scattered with beeves. First man can steady supply fresh meat's never going to have to worry."

"Wouldn't be that hard to do," Story said. "I know where there's all the cattle you could want."

"Where's that?"

"Texas. Wild Spanish longhorns cross back and forth from old Mexico, big herds of 'em, free for the taking if you can hang onto 'em. But now there's all these tame cattle running loose too. You got fifty, sixty, maybe seventy thousand Texans conscripted into the Confederate army. Had no time to make arrangements. Those without family just took their best horse or two, opened up their corral gates and let the rest of their livestock fend for itself. Some say there's two hundred thousand head roaming unattended. And longhorns are hardy. Don't need much water or taking care of at all. Buy as many as you want for a couple of bucks a head if you don't want to just go take 'em. Five for a good bull and ten for the best breeding stock they got."

"How to move 'em all the way here though?"

"Fort Worth's got the big auction yards. That's where I'd hire a crew, shape up the herd and drive 'em north up feeder trails all the way to Ogallala and then along the North Platte to the start of the Bozeman Trail. From there to here the way I just come."

"Couldn't do it now, account of the war."

"Not so sure. Confederate river navy and western armies are already defeated. Most troops both sides busy back east."

"Think you could do it?"

"'Course I could. Been sitting behind oxen since I turned eighteen. Wrangler and bullwhacker and teamster. Got my own freight company. Been all over everywhere. Here to tell you moving cattle without wagons is easier'n moving 'em with."

"You plannin' on doin' something like that?"

"Have been a little. More now I see this place and you tell me how hungry everyone is. But gold sounds easier. Find enough, let's scheme 'bout some cattle."

"Think about would you want a partner. I can't leave here but I could split the cost of buying the herd and then we could work out how many head I'd keep once you got back here. By then I'll have claim to better'n a thousand acres with all this good grass and water."

"Worth some thought," Story said. "Tell you what, we can start real small right here today. What say I leave this oxcart here with you a few days while I mule over to Alder Gulch for a look around? Use the cart to haul your goods where you want them. Then unhitch and graze the critters, fatten 'em up on this good grass."

"Could do that right enough. Got farm boys here know their way around livestock. Have to hobble 'em though or watch 'em close. Can't let 'em trample our crops."

"Should be some hobbles in the wagon somewheres. I could send one of my men up to tend 'em if you want."

"No need. Like you say, a small start to what could be big. I can fashion hobbles out of the rawhide you sold me."

"I best mount that mule then," Story said. "Burning daylight."

"I'd give you some food for the ride but 'bout the only thing come up yet is rhubarb, if you want to take a few stalks with you," Einar said. "Boil it up, it tastes pretty good and it's all you're going to find fresh around here."

By fall most of the Engebretsons' first-year crops came in better than expected. The grocery in town and another over in Alder Gulch took everything they had. With money and teamwork, each family had a rude house and a start on chicken coops and other outbuildings.

By then Nelson Story had amassed tens of thousands of dollars' worth of gold. Alder Gulch was a much richer placer strike than Grasshopper Creek. All you needed was a spot on the riverbank and a gold pan or sluice box or rocker box and your chances were as good as the next man's until the easy pickings were used up.

They talked about cattle and picked out a contiguous homestead a couple of miles west for Story. Engebretson matched ten thousand dollars of Story's money and, after a long winter, the drover set off for Texas.

Bigger houses started going up, followed by barnraisings and timber fences and corrals, and then by line shacks up in unclaimed high country so they could run cow-calf pairs in the summer.

And whenever somebody's son turned twenty-one, the family staked out another 160 acres and built it out the same way. Everybody knew about the Homestead Act by now and plenty of people were heading west. But few got this far or this remote. A high-elevation winter or two ran most of them off. And with almost two thousand of the best acres under their control, the Engebretsons never tried to discourage newcomers.

Nobody was getting rich on farming but everybody was eating well and living comfortably. And Einar was still sitting on half the gold in his poke.

Eventually he got word that Story had assembled a herd, a few wagons for supplies, one of Charlie Goodnight's chuckwagons, a cook and enough drovers and wranglers and a trail boss. After that he didn't hear much until, just after the first snowfall, Story left six hundred head in Livingston for winter feeding and drove hundreds more into Grasshopper Valley to pasture near well-stocked haymows.

Story had tales of river crossings, Indian attacks, a few troops trying without success to turn them back. A few wolves. A few losses but none of the men.

The winter wasn't too severe, though they had to chop ice every morning so the cattle could drink. The hay held out until the snowmelt. Calving barns stayed dry inside and the longhorns lived up to their reputation of easy calving. By April the pasture started greening up nicely.

At first they let the cattle go where they pleased but soon cross-fenced to prevent overgrazing.

Things went smoothly the next few years. The families and the cowherd grew in size. All the original homesteads were filed and deeded. The only controversy was whether women could be declared heads of household. Sentiment in the area was against it but the law prevailed as long as the woman was unmarried, divorced or widowed.

The community built a feedlot, slaughterhouse and meat market, doing their own butchering and wrapping so they could sell direct to anyone who was hungry.

A few years later the Utah & Northern Railway extended its narrow-gauge tracks from Idaho over Monida Pass to carry ore down to smelters near the Great Salt Lake. Unwilling to deadhead back empty, the railroad dropped the price of shipping cattle north. A new route for cattle drives, the Goodnight-Loving Trail, made it easier and safer to get longhorns from Texas to railheads, so the Engebretson clan started culling the weaker members of the herd and replacing them with better stock.

The ranches' carrying capacity was no longer limited by the amount of meat they could cut and sell or the amount of hay they'd laid up over the summer. Come fall it took just half a day to drive surplus yearlings over to the terminus at Argenta and ship them down to midwestern feedlots.

There was a natural rhythm to it all. Calving started around February and kept them busy until time to brand and castrate steers. Then they maxed out the number of cow-calf units, herding many of them up to the high country where they could graze free, monitored by adventurous youths eager to get away from home for a few months on their own in line shacks twenty-five miles apart.

When fall came they'd round 'em up, drive them back down to pasture, sort 'em by brand and drive the steers they didn't intend to keep or butcher over to the railhead. Take some time off to get in their firewood and elk and deer. Hitch big-hoofed Percherons to a wagon and go from ranch to ranch every day pitching hay on top of the snow. Stay close to the fire as much as they could and read, breed and feed until time to start all over again.

Her phone finally rings. The rarely used house phone, not her traceable cell. She picks up the receiver but, as instructed, says nothing.

All his voice says is, "Dinner tonight? My place?"

Code for I made it back okay.

"I'll bring some wine," she says, code for thank God, you asshole.

It takes almost an hour for her late-model Denali to slog through the drifts to his ranch from her college-town condo. Both dogs greet her at the gate with rowdy enthusiasm, a shaggy old Bouvier male and a younger German Shepherd female.

Hearing barking, Branch walks out to meet her. They embrace. Branch has these sensuous lips that belie the rest of his workingman's face. She attends to them with hers until she feels his road tension slipping away.

"Made pretty good time," she says.

"Reluctant to pull over much. Pretty strong smell to it, even wrapped the way it was."

"You must be exhausted," Laura says, "Hope you never have to do that again."

"Me too," Branch says. "Me either. Leave your car here."

"Blocking the gate?"

"Not expecting company. Wouldn't welcome it just now."

Arm in arm they walk past the Ithaca twelve-gauge propped in the doorway to the ranch kitchen table where he's been separating cannabis from coffee and tea, putting it into gallon ziplocs labelled with different-colored Sharpies, OGK in red for OG Kush and TW in blue for the Trainwreck. Bigger buds set aside for his own patients and the biggest and tightest for his own medicine.

He dives right back in and Laura stands behind him to administer a neck and shoulder massage before she grabs a couple of bowls from the cabinet, joins him at the table and starts sorting. "You didn't tell me there'd be so much."

"Didn't want you to worry."

"Your badboy act. Don't trouble the little woman."

"Well, I can see how smugglers might get a kick out of bringing in a heavy load. Sets the adrenaline to pumping."

"Swear to God," Laura says, "Couldn't write a law some guy wouldn't break just for the fun of it. Way you're made."

"Just men you think? Expect it's everybody. Bit of rebellion in all of us. Don't pretend there ain't none in you."

"Only when I'm right. Not like you where the wronger the stronger."

"How about Eve?"

Just like Branch to see the direction she's headed and try to tease her out of it before she can get there.

"Eve? That Eve? You buy that bullshit story? Name me one woman you know would give up a perfect home for a damn apple. Next holy book better be written by a woman. Tell it like it is, Adam strutting around full of himself, feeling all manly and badass 'cause he gets to hang out with this fascinating snake in the garden kind of reminds me of Hampton. Eve watching, wondering why in the hell, literally why in the hell, he's taking this chance. Like I do with you."

Branch laughs. "Guilty as charged."

"Went okay, though?"

"Well enough. Future looks good. Fill you in after I've had me some sleep."

"Hampton fly down, make his pitch?"

"You bet. Full-on presentation mode."

"Think Brendan's going to move up here?"

"Couldn't get a read. Wasn't just Brendan. Hamp tried to recruit the whole shitaree. Brendan's manager, some sleazeball lawyer. Time'll tell. Look over there." He points toward the corner. "Something you might be interested in."

Standing over the slumped burlap coffee sack, Laura one-hands the old Puma pocket knife Branch tosses her, flips it open and slices through the top stitching. Inside is a two mil black contractor's trash-bag. She cuts again, revealing another. A second slice and she rears back from the unleashed smell of rough-trimmed buds, strong and raw but not unpleasant. "Whoa. What's all this?"

"Pain relief for your patients."

"My grannies? We couldn't get through this in seven lifetimes."

"Doubt you'll want that much. Mixed bag, literally. The strain doesn't breed true. Guys were after high-CBD medicine that doesn't get you high. Figured you could use it. According to them—I haven't tried it—only some does that. Rest is likely average sun-grown weed. Maybe not even that. Beats me how you're gonna figure out which is which."

"Easy. Couple of grad students over in the Plant Sciences lab'd probably help me out. Supposed to be doing molecular research on pulse crops and oilseeds, but they're taking a midnight minor in herbalism."

She watches Branch bristle. It's not the first time. "Help you how?" he says.

"You'd have to see the equipment they've got. High-pressure liquid chromatography'd give me the cannabinoid breakdown but the results take a while. I've been wanting to try PCR."

"What the hell is PCR?"

"Real-time polymerase chain reaction testing. It amplifies DNA at the molecular level. Not sure it'll work for what I want, but seems like once we selected some high CBD buds with the terpenes and other traits of value we're looking for, PCR can identify the gene expressions responsible. The trick'll be to figure out how to test this much in small batches to see what matches up."

She scoops up a handful of buds and lets them trickle through her fingers back into the big sack. "I'm not sure that technology exists yet. But it'll be fun to find out."

"You're gonna just waltz in there with all this weed and ask these farts to give you a hand? You who accuse me of taking big risks? You who gives me shit about illegal quantities?"

"I'll never see the inside of that lab. I'm in Animal Science. It would look weird. I'll slip them the material on the sly."

"And they'd do this for you why?"

"They're students. They're broke. They're always scuffling for something to smoke. We'll give them the part we don't want."

"You're such a hypocrite. These guys, whoever they are, they'll be turning on their friends, telling them about this beautiful lady gives them pounds of free weed. You realize this'll all come back on me 'cause you know, somebody gets interested, they're going to look for the boyfriend. You're putting everybody in jeopardy. You, me, Brendan, Hampton. Sometimes I don't get you at all."

"Relax, Branch. I know what I'm doing."

"They get busted they'll mew like kittens and give us up."

"Ease up. They're the most harmless guys in the world. Give me up? They'd die first. But if it makes you feel better I'll dole it out an ounce at a time. Just I'd feel better if I didn't have pounds sitting around my apartment, you know?"

"Keep it here with me. Might as well be hanged for a sheep as a lamb. I can whittle it down some, sell shake and popcorn buds dirt cheap to my patients living on welfare and SSI while you and your buddies push the frontiers of science."

Laura drags the bag to the table and then rummages through Branch's kitchen cabinets for a big colander. She starts separating buds from stems and shake. "Seeds here," she says.

Most people would complain, seeds drawing energy and potency away from the buds and the smoke. But not her. She's ranch. "How cool is that?" she says.

"Thought you might approve," Branch says. "Play around some, see what you come up with."

She takes two more bowls from the cupboard, tosses seeded buds in one bowl and loose seeds in another, and stuffs unseeded weed into gallon baggies. "Brew me up a double cap, will you? Then go to bed. You're starting to fade. Get your rest. I'm staying over, sort this all out. Enough seeds here for a controlled double-blind."

"Wasting your time," Branch says. "I can get you some primo Dutch F-one seeds my next order out of England."

"Where's the challenge? What if those guys were onto something? I can pick up where they left off, stand on their shoulders. Stabilize a high CBD strain? That's sure worth reaching for. What science is all about. Revolutionize medicine. Leave you tokin' folks in the dust, fun though you be when you're toasted. Where's my vape?"

"In the closet. Small bedroom. I'll get it."

"Rest easy, Branch."

Branch yawns and shrugs. "Overhead shelf. Take the penlight." He reaches into a drawer and switches on a narrow green beam. "They're sleeping," he says.

Laura walks down the dark hall. It looks like a nightvision ghost-hunt reality show.

She opens the door to a converted bedroom. Reflective mylar lines the walls. Pandacloth covers the only window. Metal halide lights, reflectors and ducting loom dark over seedlings and vegging plants. She swings the emerald beam around. The plants all look great. Man knows what he's doing.

Laura reaches high in the closet for her woven hemp bag, blows the dust off it and glides back into the kitchen where she opens the freezer and takes out her glycerine-filled vapor tamer and mouthpiece. She clears a space on the table, unbags her vaporizer and plugs it in. While it warms up she attaches the wand to one end of some surgical tubing. The icy blue vapor tamer goes on the other end.

She locates a nice sinsemilla bud, inhales its aroma, twists off the stem. "Bit moist yet. Couldn't be much fresher. Should I be worried about mold?"

"Get it out of the bag first off, air it out some. Then burp it every day as it cures." Branch says, leaning back.

"Too damp for a grinder," Laura says. "Hand me that cutting board, will you?"

The Puma's still open so she rock-chops the bud and knifeblades it into the flared end of the vaporizer wand. Pushes it onto the vape's ceramic heater, takes a long, gentle pull and then slides the wand back off the glass. She spaces out two more inhalations before turning off the glowing vape. Disassembles the kit back into the hemp bag and returns the vapor tamer to the freezer.

"Might just do," she says.

"Don't get your hopes up," Branch says. "Nobody's isolated its high CBD phenotype yet."

"Back-crossing just takes time and good records. It's all about the herd, not the steer."

"Look, you're a great caregiver and all, but get real. Isolating and propagating specific traits? That's complicated stuff. Guys who've succeeded been at it for decades."

Laura doesn't much care for his tone. "Suppose breeding a plant's somehow harder'n breeding Angus?"

"I'm just saying..."

"Listen, bud. Don't even try to school me in genetics. Back when you were a kid, ever draw straws with your friends, see who wins a prize?"

Branch's face clouds for a moment. "All the time. For a while."

"Straws I was drawing that age were full of bull semen."

"Bull what?"

"Flash-froze 'em in liquid nitrogen so I could carry 'em around one bull to the next in a tank on my back. Older brother called it my testisicle. Was years before I knew what he was talking about."

"So how'd you..." Branch pauses.

"Want I tell you? Or just show you?"

He stares.

"You know what they say about silence. Get down on all fours. Assume the position."

"What, now?"

"Now would be a good time."

# CHAPTER NINE

# GREENRUSH BOYS

Brendan and Natty wait in Natty's apartment. The living room is stacked with boxes of energy drinks. Brendan's face is healing, reconstructive surgery on his eye socket giving him an even more hooded look. Natty, stoking a three-foot bong, wears a long, loose unbleached painter smock over Belgian linen drawstring pants. Made to hold big dreadlock nests, his knit rasta cap in the colors of the Jamaican flag flops over his forehead like a tie-died Shiitake mushroom.

Sporting a snap-button western shirt and stiff new Tony Lama ostrich boots, Johnny Legal arrives straight from the San Jose airport to report on his Montucky trip.

Enthusiastic, he jumps right in like it's a courtroom summation. "Tell you what, Hampton wasn't just woofin.' What a couple of weeks.

He's going balls to the wall. Figures to pretty much own medical cannabis statewide. Barely a million people up there, he might just pull it off. Got folks testifying in front of senators, law enforcement, mayors, interim legislative committees, even the local head of the DEA. Goddamn full court press. Drafting up wording, bills and regulations for when the lawmakers get together in a year or so."

Natty says, "What's the law like now?" Knows it cold but wants Bear to hear the lawyer perspective.

"Caregiver grows six plants per patient, can sell each one an ounce at a time. Patient can grow six more for himself."

Brendan says, "What about restrictions, requirements? Collectives, cooperatives, nonprofits?"

"None of that. They're all about free enterprise and individual rights," Johnny says. "Don't see profit as a crime."

"What's it take to get a card?" Natty says, knowing that too.

"Just be a resident is all. Need a phone or power bill and a rental or lease agreement to get your Montucky driver's license. Then hunt up a pain doctor to sign off."

"All there is to it?" says Natty.

"Couple of forms. Write in who you want for a caregiver. Whole business took me maybe an hour and a half."

Natty says, "What happens if I write you in but you're not really a caregiver?"

"I am then," Johnny says. "State mails me a form to sign. But I better have an ounce ready anytime you want. You can't buy from anyone but me so if I fail to perform you kick me to the curb. They give you a change-of-caregiver form and you write in someone else."

"S'pose I name Bear as my caregiver," Natty says, "and he comes through for me. I tell my friends 'bout this great medicine he's got and they all write him in, he can grow six more for each?"

Johnny says, "Better'n that if you're a slimeball MLM guy hip to the magic of downlines like some lowlifes I know." He winks. "Even if your guy's going to be the one providing the medicine, you tell your friends to write you in as caregiver instead. 'Cause then you get to grow the six for each patient but he gets to grow and sell you the same amount because you share the obligation to provide all of them an ounce every time they run dry, whether you both grow or you buy it all from him."

This is news to Natty. "But that means..." He's calculating.

Johnny beats him to the punch. "Ten people write you in, you can grow sixty plants for them and six for yourself. Even if your upline has only you as a patient, he can grow sixty-six more plants plus six for himself. And of course if he has ten other downlines like you, well, you get the picture."

Natty says, "Work the same way for sales?"

"Absolutely."

"Hungry MLM guys and weed," Natty says. "Two of my favorite things. You boys see the implications? No multilevel marketing comp plan comes close. It's exponential. Everybody in the downline grows and buys for everybody below him? That's insane. Guys at the top wouldn't even need very many legs; just build 'em long. Need a calculator but you'd be at hundreds of plants and dozens of ounces in no time. Then thousands and hundreds. You sure the law says that, Johnny?"

"It's not what it says, it's what it doesn't. Law doesn't run a full page and it got more votes than the president. Only a few provisions. Big one is every caregiver's obliged to grow and stock enough to provide for his patients and, if they're caregivers, their patients too. You can't hire help. Caregiver's a personal relationship you gotta fulfill yourself."

"Get it how the downline works," Natty says. "How 'bout the upline?"

"That part's cute too. You grow more'n you can use to where you're about to go over your possession limit, you can sell it off to your caregiver. Have to, in fact, don't want to be a criminal. So really you can all be selling to each other except you've got to honor the chain of command. You can only sling to your caregiver or your patients. Skipping over anybody's the only crime."

Natty says, "Avon, Amway, Herbalife, eat your heart out. You too, Mary Kay. I can modify our Crave marketing plan to lock it in just like that. Hack the software to announce anyone's got too much or too little. Real-time notifications to everybody in between. Anyone implementing something like that?"

"Nope. I don't think anybody's looking that far ahead. Folks trying to take away customers from each other. Some selling out the back door. Shortage of pot and pot doctors hold things back."

Natty says to Brendan, "What we've been talking about with xCeed? Tie these two together. Production gets rolling we could sure help move it."

Johnny says, "Would reduce dependence on Hampton's distribution too. One less question mark. Probably a dozen other ways to game the system."

Natty smiles. "Must be tough on law enforcement."

"Paralyzed, what I hear," says Johnny Legal. "Not much to enforce. Plus they got a pretty big meth problem up there to focus on. Seems like they're leaving the weed alone."

Brendan says, "How many patients can a caregiver have?"

Johnny says, "Many as they can provide for. They call it holding cards up there. Hundred patients is a hundred cards. What I don't think they get is you don't have to hold those cards yourself. Could be a downline of twenty, each holding five cards. Either way you can buy or sell seventeen kilos a day, cop sitting right there, legal as you please. Least that's what the lawyer in me says. Hardly busting any medical marijuana people yet and when they do it's for stupid stuff. Limits we're talking about have never been tested in court."

Brendan says, "Feds might have something to say about that."

Johnny says, "Yeah, but you take that risk anywhere. Most folks there think as long as they comply with state laws and nothing crosses a border either way, feds can't touch 'em. Or won't, anyway. Hampton's already got me writing up proposed legislation and private grower-to-grower agreements. Don't underestimate how much they care about states' rights and self-determination. Or how little they like federal interference. Don't see how Washington has the right to tell Montucky what to do. Give you an idea, a recent bill would've made the county sheriff the highest law of the land. Even FBI or DEA or Homeland Security'd need to clear a raid beforehand. Sheriff refuses, no explanation necessary, no invasion, no recourse. Didn't get the votes but got more'n you might think and it'll likely be back. You imagine that being debated and passed out of committee in the People's Republic of California?"

"So what's your plan?" says Natty.

"Pretty much the way Hampton laid it out. Secret facility, big, state of the art. Best of everything. Weed I can't raise myself I'll sneak up from here. This guy needs us. He succeeds, he'll drive out the little fish. But his whole deal falls apart if he doesn't have product. We got him by the short and curlies. Cash out in a couple of years, sell him the whole op. You guys want to run your MLM scam in the meantime I'll keep you supplied. Best not let him know about it though."

Brendan says, "Thought Branch'd be running the grow."

Johnny says. "Who needs the cowboy? You have a problem with that, him kin and all?"

Brendan says, "Who decided? You or Hampton?"

"Hampton asked my opinion."

"Long time since that scudder needed me to step in for him. And I wasn't crazy about the way Hampton's been using him anyway. Had my doubts it'd work out. Gotta say though it's snakebelly low on both your parts. Man's word's not good I don't have much use for him. But I got nothing to do with the cultivation part. My deal's the gym. Less I know who does what the better."

Johnny says, "You got that right."

"Not saying I won't back Hampton down if he doesn't do right by Branch. Might kick his ass a little. But I won't fuck the deal up for you on account of it."

"Brought you back some pictures." Johnny pops open his battered courtroom attache case and fans out glossies.

"Six stories," he says. "Fifty-five thousand square feet. We say yes and Hampton'll close. Offer's already accepted but inspections and contingency clauses enough he can still bail if we turn him down. Otherwise he's ready to rock. Has urban renewal grant agreements in place, low-income loans, carpenters and plumbers and electricians standing by. Cut a check tomorrow for a deepwater culture system. We just got to let him know. Cut you one tomorrow too, Bear, starting with your relocation costs."

"So you're in?" says Natty.

"Nut-deep. Even without Bear if necessary. It's that good. I'm on retainer and studying for the Montucky bar, even though I won't practice openly. My name'll never be on any of these documents. Hide behind attorney-client privilege."

Brendan shuffles photos of an impressive facade and indoor shots of ornate rooms with tile and hardwood floors, mahogany paneling, big steamrooms and baths. "I get my name on the gym, run it how I please? Do everything I want?"

"You bet."

"Let's do it then," Brendan says. "The green rush boys saddle up. 'Less Natty sees something I don't."

Johnny says, "How about it, Natty? Opportunity for you as well?"

"More'n you know. But not quite the one Hampton has in mind. He's no fool but I'm smarter. Haven't been sittin' around with my thumb up my ass either. You guys do what you're talkin' about. Brendan and I'll sit down and figure out if we want to do anything with the MLM. But the rest of my plan'll be on my own. I'll be real public and you don't want to get mixed up in it."

His gaze drifts over to Brendan. "You know, Bear, maybe you were right. Might not be much us for a while. It's been a good run and I'll always be in your corner. But you guys're gonna want to pretend you don't know me. I'll be up the road in Duckburg. Perfect town for me. Lots of diversity. Radicals, gays, college ecofreaks, stoners. Lots of stoners. Great place for my new act. For my new product."

Brendan says, "New product?"

Natty gives them a showman's pause. "Me."

He sweeps the rasta cap off his head and frisbees it across the room in a grand gesture to reveal... nothing. Bald as a baby's butt, all that Jesus hair gone.

He clasps his hands in a pious pose. "Reinvented myself. Like it? Just got back from the courthouse. Changed my name too. Turns out you can call yourself pretty much whatever you want."

Johnny Legal raises his eyes to the ceiling. "You go by what now?"

"Lost the Nathaniel. It's just Nat. New middle name's Thai so you can still call me Natty."

Natty gives it an actor's pause before he reaches for his party bong. After a long bubbling hit he passes it to Johnny and folds his hands in a pious pose. "New last name is Christ. Natty Christ. Nat T. Christ. Nat Thai Christ. N.T. Christ. Anyway you say it, I'm gonna be notorious. Guy they'll love to hate. Except for the hipsters who dig outrageous. Guarantee you one thing. Nobody going to forget me."

Johnny Legal stares at him. Brendan stares at him.

"Pronounce it Crist if you're so fucking sensitive."

"Jesus H. Christ," is all Brendan can say.

"Was my first choice. But it's taken."

# CHAPTER TEN

# STANDOFF

Brendan's summer vacation and winter break visits to Paradise Valley took on a comfortable routine. On the way north each time he'd phone from an hour away to make sure the boy was ready.

He always was. Brendan'd switch off his rig but leave the key in the ignition. In the west it's rude to walk right up and knock, so he'd call from the yard, "Hello, the house."

Hattie'd answer the door, give Brendan a quick wordless hug and go back to what she was doing. She left everything up to them. Plenty of time to catch up later.

Branch'd grab his neatly packed gear and they'd be out of there. Adios Church Universal and Triumphant. Hello camping, roadtrips, hunting, fishing, skiing, snowboarding, ascending Montucky's great peaks, skydiving, the rodeo circuit, ghost towns: whatever they felt like doing.

Sometimes they'd just take aimless drives, stopping wherever they took a fancy. They'd make a game out of it. Whenever they reached an intersection or even an appealing dirt road, Branch would silently point left or right, straight ahead, or sometimes back behind them. That's the direction they'd go. Even if they passed the same place three times in a row, Brendan never complained or offered a suggestion.

Or they'd just hike away from the church compound, upriver into Yellowstone Park with everything they needed for a week or so carefully arranged in Brendan's rust-colored custom Gregory backpack. They stayed out in the woods as long as they cared to. He taught Branch how to look to the sky, watch the clouds and test the wind for weather hints.

Brendan taught the boy things he didn't know he knew and didn't know how he knew. He even spoke different, from an older time.

One day early in Brendan's fifth Paradise Valley summer, they drove west into logging country past a century-old sawmill to the Ruana Knife Works in Bonner, where he bought the boy a small skinning knife. Ten miles further up the Blackfoot they stopped at Johnsrud Park, climbed a cliff above the river and searched until Brendan found the sort of flinty rock he was looking for. He showed Branch how to strike the rock with the spine of the Ruana to knap off thin flakes.

Once their pockets were full they continued up Highway 200, their hunting knives sheathed on their belts, as the landscape widened into gorgeous green Potomac Valley ranchland and then narrowed again to rejoin the Blackfoot.

Further upriver they stopped for lunch at Trixi's Antler Saloon where they sidled up to a long bar emblazoned with local ranch brands burned into the wood with hot irons. Cowboys, wilderness guides and fishermen made room for them, sliding whiskey shots and schooners of beer out of the way, eyeing the boy to see how well he could climb up on a steel tractorseat barstool.

Branch swung aboard with ease and acted as if this sort of thing happened every day. But his grin gave him away.

The barmaid came out of the kitchen and brought them menus.

Brendan glanced quickly at his and said, "Hungry enough for a steak?"

"Sure," Branch said. The church had loosened up its prohibition on eating animals but the practice was still rare and the meat was not.

"We'll split a 32-ounce T-bone medium rare," Brendan said to the barmaid. "And run the fries through the gutter. You have Moose Drool on tap?"

"You betcha, hon," she said. She smiled at the boy. "Will that be one or two?"

Branch looked flustered.

"Just the one," Brendan said. "For now. They call him Branch, so let's start him out with a bourbon and branch. But hold the bourbon."

The barmaid laughed. "He's right cute."

Brendan didn't say much before the food came. He just sidelong watched Branch sip water and listen in on all the loud, jovial and sometimes rowdy fragments of conversation up and down the bar and over at the pool table.

Branch's eyes widened when their plates came, one after the other, fresh-baked bread with big scoops of butter on the side, followed by large salads and piles of french fries laden with brown gravy. They really popped when the barmaid set a giant platter directly in front of him. It was covered from edge to edge with a heavily marbled steak two inches thick.

The barmaid handed the boy a steak knife but Brendan said, "Let's see what kind of edge that Ruana of yours has. Carve me off a slab of that steer, would you pardner?"

The bar quieted down and Branch could feel men watching as he unsheathed his skinner.

Branch looked at the meat and looked at his knife and then looked up at Brendan.

"Best hold the beef good with your fork in your fist while you slice so it don't slide away," Brendan said. "Cut right alongside the bone."

The knife glided through the meat. Reddish juices ran.

"Now fork me over the big piece with the bone," Brendan said, pushing his fries to one side. "If what's left ain't enough for you I'll give you some of mine."

Branch stared at the thick pound of meat in front of him. Friendly laughter ran down the bar. A grizzled old-timer said, "Kid's growing up right."

"Shitfire," said the man next to him, "I'd've turned out all right too, Pa, you'd given me a knife like that when I was his age."

The next man down said, "Would've took more'n that."

Halfway through the meal Branch slowed and Brendan said, "Here, wash it down with this," and gave the boy a sip of his Moose Drool. The barmaid just smiled as Branch tried to act nonchalant at the taste of the thick, dark beer.

"Box those up for you?" the barmaid said when their eating slowed.

"You betcha," Brendan said.

"Room for dessert? The apple pie's homemade. The a la mode's Wilcoxson's."

Branch said, "No way."

Brendan called out, "Anybody got a good-sized dog? Hell of a bone to let go to waste. But I ain't into feeding bears."

Plenty of takers. Brendan ripped it away from the meat, wrapped it in a napkin and pushed it toward the barmaid. "We'll let the sweetheart of the rodeo here decide."

On the way out to the pickup, Branch said, "Can we make camp early today, Uncle Brendan? It's nice here and I'd just like to relax."

"Sure, Branch. Passed us up a fishing access site on the Blackfoot a few miles back. Close to the road so we shouldn't have to worry none about moose or bear."

"You're kidding, right?"

"Got your phone? Look up the video of a spike elk chasing a motorcycle right along this highway."

"What's an elk want with a motorcycle?"

Brendan laughed. "He was in rut."

At Branch's blank look Brendan said, "Rutting season, right around this time of year when you hear elk bugle? You savvy rut?"

"Heard of in a rut. Never heard of in rut."

"It's like being in heat but for boys. Probably hoping to hump that scooter."

Branch started to chuckle, stopped, and then broke out laughing. "Just got a mind's-eye view of that."

They pitched their tent a respectful distance from the fisherman taking advantage of the afternoon mayfly and caddisfly hatch.

After securing their food in the truck, Brendan said, "Want to see a little more woodlore?"

"Can I use my knife?"

"'Course you can," Brendan said. "Let's see can we snare us something before dark." He showed the boy how to make small animal snares out of branches and twine. Once the snares were set riverside he suggested, "Find us a good tree uphill we can lean against while we wait."

Finally a rabbit triggered one snare. They walked down and Brendan showed Branch how to quickly and humanely dispatch it with a single sharp blow of the knife's butt cap to its head.

Branch practiced on the dead animal until he had it down.

Next, Brendan showed Branch how to behead and eviscerate the rabbit without damaging meat.

Branch wasn't squeamish. He took the gutted rabbit down to the stream on his own, thumbed it open and rinsed it off.

Brendan sent the boy off to gather twigs and scoop punk out of rotten logs. They pyramided punk and twigs on a cleared spot of ground and built a circle of rocks around it. Then Brendan reached into his pack's side pocket and removed an ornate old tin coughdrop box featuring two oval portraits of bearded men.

"My tinderbox," Brendan said. "Pretty much rainproof, way the top extends down over the edge. When we get back we'll make you one. Always want it with you when you're in the woods. Real big difference can you make a fire."

Brendan removed a thin metal rod and a piece of charred cotton. "No shame in carrying a cigarette lighter, but you never know when it might fail. A good firesteel and some well-prepared charcloth'll keep you safe and happy. 'Cause who wants to eat a raw rabbit? Not me, 'cept in emergencies."

"Not me," Branch said, eyeing it. "But I don't want to eat a cooked one either. I'm still full."

"Sometimes you go days or weeks without fresh meat. Got to take it when you find it. We had more time, we could dry and smoke the meat slow and add berries to make pemmican won't rot or spoil. But that's a lesson for another time. We'll roast 'er up slow and have a late supper after we've pitched our tent. It's all kinds of wrong to kill an animal and not eat it. We don't do this for fun. Make us some stew with what we don't eat tonight and that leftover steak tomorrow with some watercress from the creek and whatever else we can find looks good. Get lucky, find us a beaver dam, it might not be too late in the year to dig up some morels where trees've been chewed down. Gimme your knife."

With the Ruana Brendan trimmed off a piece of cotton. "When we get back I'll show you how to make charcloth. There's a trick to it." He put it on top of the tinder pyramid. "You still have that flint we chipped off this morning? You'd carry that in your tinderbox too."

Branch dug into his pocket.

Brendan showed him how to hold the flint at an angle and strike the firesteel above the charcloth. Sparks flew and lit the cloth, which just glowed at first but then burst into flame, igniting the tinder.

Following Brendan's directions, Branch carefully added twigs and then small branches to the fire without collapsing the pyramid.

"Long as you've got your flint and your steel and your charcloth in your tinderbox you can always make a fire, even if it's wet out. Keep you warm, keep any wolves away, cook what you catch, stay alive."

Branch was all eyes and ears.

"Go find us some green wood that's thick as your thumb so it can stand up to the fire. We don't want it to burn. Want it to hold the meat out of the flame and coals and smoke it up good."

When the boy brought limbs back for inspection, Brendan picked out some the right size and said, "Now whittle four of them smooth about yea long; don't leave no shavings sticking out to ignite. Another one real skinny twice as long or more for a skewer. And do watch yourself with that knife. Hold the stick well back. Can't take you back to your mom with whittled fingers."

While Branch trimmed, Brendan built up the fire and let it start to burn down to coals. Then he showed the lad how to poke the four smooth pieces of wood into the ground so they formed X-braces on either side of the flames.

Brendan took the skinner and said, "So let me tell you what makes your skinning knife different. Can do a lot of things but the blade's designed for separating hide from skin 'cause you don't want to be eatin' fur. Has to have a little flexibility to follow the contours of what you're skinning but still strong enough to hack through bone if you don't have a bigger knife with you. You want that fur off before you start cooking, else it burns and makes the meat smell bad, same's your own hair would."

Something awful passed over Branch's face.

Brendan patted the boy's shoulder in a brief gesture. "Terrible sorry, Branch. Wasn't thinkin.'"

"It's okay. Now," Branch said.

"Besides," Brendan went on, "We're going to use this hide for something else. Every part of an animal has a use and it's a sin against the natural order of things not to use it all."

"Maybe a rabbit's foot for luck?"

"Don't see where's the luck in that. And it's not respectful, boy. You honor what you kill. Want some animal like a moose or a bear carrying your foot around for luck?"

Branch said, "My turn, say I wasn't thinking." He fondled the rough textures of the elk antler handle. "I love this knife, Uncle Brendan. The way it fits in my hand. Did you see how those men in the saloon perked up when you said Ruana, like it was a magic word? The way they looked at it?"

"Old Rudy Ruana's famous in these parts. Figured out how to forge indestructible knifes cut out of huge circular saw blades recycled from that sawmill we went by this morning. Turned eighty before he retired so there's a half century of his knives still used every hunting season. And his family's still making 'em too. Couple of those guys at the bar knew enough to give it the eagle eye, see was it one of Rudy's."

"Is it?"

"Hell yeah. They still make 'em kind of the same, and if it was just for using I might've gone for a new one. But someday you have a son or daughter, you'll want to pass it along so I thought the real thing'd be better. Original condition too, near as I can tell. They buy back old ones when they can and rebuild 'em, but I don't think this is one of those."

"Made me feel proud back there. Made me feel important."

"You've got you there a smallish weapon 'cause your hands ain't that big yet. But that don't make it any less a knife. You had to, you could quarter out a deer or an elk with this thing. Just takes longer and you'd have to hammer it with something to chop through any bigger bones. Mind if I take it and give you a lesson? Don't want to screw up the meat because there ain't that much on a rabbit, but that makes it good practice. I'll start the skinning and then guide your hand. Watch close 'cause your next catch you're gonna do it by yourself. Okay?"

Branch watched Brendan cut off the haunches, careful to remove intact the tendons that led to the jumping muscles. Then, together, they halved the rest along the spine and then slid clean between the skin and the meat.

Brendan raked some of the coals to the side, scraped the pelts' insides, and placed them on the coals meat-side down for only a few seconds, just enough to sear and sizzle away the remaining flesh without blackening the fur. Setting the matched skins aside, he said, "Had us more time you could just hang these to dry but either way you don't want your possibles bag rotting. 'Cause that's what you're making here. But let's get our food going first."

Brendan showed Branch how to skewer the haunches and body. Then the boy placed the skewers on the X-braces over the coals to roast.

While the meal cooked, Brendan showed Branch how to align the skin halves fur side out and use the Ruana's needle-sharp point to awl evenly spaced edge holes top and bottom. Branch threaded one tendon through the lower holes to fashion a pouch. Then, after a question, he threaded part of the other tendon topside for a drawstring and used the rest for beltloops in the back.

They dined from their fingers and Branch, wearing his possibles bag and his Ruana sheath proudly, proclaimed it the best meal he'd ever eaten. Brendan, a long ways from agreeing, gave him a game nod.

The next morning they broke camp and, a few miles down the highway, followed a long, rough dirt road up into the vast Bob Marshall Wilderness. They parked at the Monture Creek trailhead and packed in.

A half hour later they arrived at a beautiful creekside meadow camping area where Brendan said, "See that metal thing? It's bearproof and the bears know it. Put all our food in there while I set up the tent. You're out in the woods and don't have something like that, shinny up a tree with a rope, crawl out on a stout limb and hang your pack way off the ground. Don't wait to do it lest a bear get to it first. I'll put up the tent."

But the tent was only halfway up when Brendan's hair stood on end. He spun around with a tent stake in his hand to see a large grizzly at the edge of the clearing.

"Damn it. Don't look back," Brendan shouted at Branch. "Don't look at me. Just go like hell. Climb a tree and stay there till I call you down."

Several long, fast strides squared Brendan up directly in front of the bear, who reared up tall.

Both animals glared.

"Bite me," Brendan said.

Something passed between them. The staredown lingered.

Brendan advanced on the grizzly in slow, measured paces.

The bear dropped to all fours, pawed the air in what looked like acknowledgment, and ambled off.

Hair still bristling, Brendan turned and looked up at Branch. "You secured all our food?"

"Mostly. Held back some trail mix for a snack."

"Damn your eyes, boy," Brendan shouted. "Snack for who? I tell you do something I expect it done. You dassn't fuck around out here."

"Sorry, Uncle Brendan."

"Sorry don't cut it. Get down here and stash the rest. Immediately. That ol' boy smells anything out and comes back, I can't fend him off a second time without it gets real ugly."

Once that was done, Brendan said, calmer now, "Finish with the tent. I best build us a fire pronto."

The next day, safely out of bear country on their way back to Paradise Valley, Brendan said, "About yesterday. Sorry I barked at you like that."

"Sorry you had to," Branch said. "Completely my fault. Heard you but didn't listen. Never happen again."

"I don't know what you could see up that tree or couldn't. And I'm guessing it's an adventure you'd be tempted to tell. But there's things about me I don't let out. So don't you ever mention it to anybody, not even a word to your mom or some girl you're trying to impress. Nor to me. Ever."

"But why, Brendan? You were a hero. I've never seen anything—"

"We're done talking about it. You're hearing me this time? Not just listening?"

"Yes, sir, Uncle Brendan."

"Don't fuck up again. Got me? I ain't saying it twice."

"'Kay. Got you. Loud and clear. You're the boss."

# CHAPTER ELEVEN

# GENETICS

Laura's Hyalite condo is small and cheaply built but it's been hers since she started grad school. Her family bought it trashed and cheap when real estate collapsed. Moonlighting Tumbling E ranch hands who'd do anything for her cowboyed it into shape during the off weeks between roundup and hunting season. Close to campus, it's big enough for one, maybe two in a pinch if she ever figures out the roommate thing.

Powdery snowclouds swirl outside her window—left, right, up, down. It's a full-on January blizzard. Near gale-force winds bang double-hung panes. Her stovepipe is howling.

She usually does fieldwork over at the Red Bluff Research Center a dozen miles this side of Branch's spread north of Pony. But this morning, snowed in, she stares at her phone, waiting for the biggest call of her career. She gives her dissertation, *Genomic Enhancements to Expected Progeny Differences: Revolutionizing the Cowherd*, one more look-through for talking points, but the words are just a blur.

Once again, back to her blog.

As Montucky Territory grew, folks migrated away from gold claims. Went north and then east. Settled into wider and warmer lower-elevation valleys where rivers pushed fingers through productive soil. Landholders who left the Grasshopper Valley sold out to the extended Engebretson clan.

Not much demand for produce then so the family cut back their farming to only what they needed for themselves. They put all the energy into ranching instead. But rangy longhorns were wrong for the place, more suited to sparse Texas scrublands than Montucky abundance. The meat was stringy and tough and there wasn't enough of it.

So Einar Engebretson and his sons started looking into other breeds just as Aberdeen Angus were first imported from the Scottish highlands. A team of younger Engebretsons took a train to the Chicago stockyards, glad to get out of Montucky and see the world, partying all the way in Pullmans and lounge cars. Stocky, heavy-shouldered Angus, both black and red, looked like superior beef producers, and it wasn't milk the boys were after.

Angus seemed real easy to handle. Best of all, they didn't have those terrible horns. It wasn't that longhorns would intentionally attack you. But if you were doing something harmless next to one when he decided to scratch his flank, he'd swing his head and open you up. Fact is, Angus had no horns at all on their big squared-off heads. And they seemed even calmer than longhorns, especially considering they were in a noisy, crowded stockyard.

The boys liked what they saw, picked out a few cows to see how purebred Angus might do back home, but mostly chose big, sturdy bulls to crossbreed with their longhorns. They paid cash on the barrelhead and supervised the loading onto the cattle car. Then they boarded and got themselves loaded for a long whiskey'd-up trainride home.

The families cross-bred a couple of generations and didn't like what they saw. But the purebred Angus calves came out nice and grew nicer. Every Angus, red or black, thrived on the lush pasture.

The boys returned to the midwest along with some more experienced elders because this was going to be a big purchase. After close inspection they bought up the best Angus bulls they could find and as many Angus cows as they could afford.

Back home they slaughtered or sold off every longhorn and every crossbreed within a year. Then they consolidated all the family brands into a single identity, the Tumbling E. They were making their stand.

From that moment the Engebretson clan stayed purebred.

By the late 1880s the Tumbling E ranch had the largest pure Angus cowherd north of the Red and west of the Divide, and the Engebretsons were founding members of the American Aberdeen-Angus Breeders' Association. Like most Angus breeders of the time, they didn't differentiate between black and red cattle, otherwise genetically identical except that red was a recessive gene denoting no weakness or other recessive trait.

When World War I came along, with everybody preoccupied and many of the smarter guys fighting overseas, the association made a long-term mistake. They split over whether red Angus were inferior. The members decided they were, with the Engebretson clan leading a vocal minority. From then on the association would register only black Angus.

It was a sudden and unexpected hardship for most RA ranchers, as the guys running reds called themselves. They couldn't sell their cattle for much and there was no demand for the services of their bulls.

But Laura's great grandfather saw it as a buying opportunity. Generations of experience told him hide color didn't mean squat, so he bought up the best red bloodlines he could find for pennies on the dollar. Breeding was his main interest but the money then was in the cow-calf operation, selling yearling steers. Butcher one and fork into its rib-eye, no way could you tell did its hide used to be red or black. Buying 'em cheap and selling 'em dear worked fine for him and his boys, so he gradually and quietly sold off his black Angus.

Other than the Tumbling E, few cattlemen remained in the Pioneers. The Engebretsons leased sixteen thousand acres summer grazing on the same government land they'd been running stock on for years anyway. But now it was guaranteed, and it was cheap.

The operation ran like clockwork and was just the right size. They were sitting on plenty of cash.

The only difficulty seemed to be outside their control. Omaha and Chitown feedlots were in the heart of black Angus country. Their buyers subscribed to the belief that black is better, or at least pretended to when negotiating with hayseeds. "How can you expect us to pay the same market rates as we'd give for association-accredited Angus?" they insisted.

What the hay, the boys said, full of themselves. They asked for a family business meeting and suggested they buy a controlling interest in a feedlot and become operators.

After a lot of discussion and a vote they were told, "See how much it would take."

They made contact with some people they'd met in Chicago who arranged a meeting with a broker who was willing to come up and check out their operation before making discreet inquiries.

After he returned, impressed with the Tumbling E and its red Angus cowherd, he located a small feedlot whose owner wanted to retire but whose employees wanted to stay. Eventually the deal was done and restless young Jimmy Earl went to Chicago to manage it and taste the pleasures of the city. He'd grown up cutting a wide swath with a horse-drawn hay mower and he was eager to cut another through the big city. He figured to do his part to make the Roaring Twenties roar.

Newspaper clippings he sent back home sure made it seem like he knew how.

The boom years of the early Twenties were favorable for red Angus. Steak houses stopped referring to Angus as black. Prices in the store and at the feedlot were rising.

The families grew and thrived. With good breeding practices their cowherd quality steadily improved.

When the Depression hit they saw opportunities to expand their holdings. Some neighboring ranches were failing. But everybody knew the Engebretsons would buy them out at a fair price before they'd see a single acre default to out-of-state bankers. Always had. Always would.

By then the Tumbling E included a much bigger clan of brothers and sisters and in-laws and cousins consolidating their efforts on separate spreads. They never feuded. It was all about cooperation.

Branding and roundup time were extended family affairs. Starting at calving they shared scrupulous notes—birth weight, wean weight and yearling weight—as well as carcass traits at harvest. At breeding time they loaned each other their best animals, caring more about the entire cowherd than who owned what.

In the decade of prosperity after the second world war the Engebretsons and six other extended families started a national breed association exclusively for red Angus. Far smaller than the black association, they figured their advantage was to be way more data-driven. Register an animal with them and you better submit comprehensive information about that animal's development twice a year as well as all its progeny's. Miss one report and your critter was out and so were you.

Ranching was getting pretty scientific by then anyway, with sophisticated tracking and better land management practices. All but the most conservative ranchers saw plenty of benefit. They liked to joke over coffee in a diner or hoisting schooners in a saloon that it was time to take the bull by the horns 'cept Angus had none.

Profits soared. Artificial insemination and shared record-keeping made Angus a household name for superior beef. All the Engebretson households plowed their money back into the business.

By the time Laura was born, the Tumbling E was one of the leading red Angus seedstock producers, running over a thousand cow-calf units, hundreds of replacement heifers, and more than a hundred sires, all backed by generations of selective breeding. And the selective breeding wasn't just the cattle. It was the families as well. They'd all been shaped by the place they'd been shaping. It was in their blood.

Her phone rings promptly at three. "Hello, Ms. Engebretson? This is Claude deKoop. I'm vice president of Human Relations for Pfizer in our Kalamazoo office. With your permission I'd like this to be a round-table discussion."

"Certainly, sir," she said.

"Splendid. You're on speakerphone here. With me is Dr. Claude Behrens, in charge of all our genomic projects and a world-recognized expert; Diane Sheldon–Ayers, our divisional head of marketing; and Sreekanth Subramanian, our senior director of technical services."

Laura says, "Hi, everyone. Nice to meet you all, virtually."

deKoop says, "We can, of course Ms. Engebretson, discuss anything you'd like, so feel free to redirect the conversation whenever you wish. But, if I may, I'd suggest we start with a review of your internship. It'll give us a shared context for talking about future opportunities with Pfizer. Once we have an idea of where your preferences lie, we'll follow up with any questions you might have. If everything goes okay, we'll put our heads together and, well before you graduate, submit an offer we hope you'll accept."

"That sounds great," Laura says, stretching her arms over her head and yawning. Long night before with Branch, avoiding any mention of today.

deKoop says she's the best intern they've ever had. Brought so much to the table with the once-in-a-lifetime opportunity to genotype every head on the Tumbling E at no cost and use them as a validation herd against their black Angus research herd so they could recalibrate more accurately.

Then, he continues, she displayed real marketing savvy in negotiating full below-cost testing for the entire Red Angus Association of America cowherd in exchange for displaying every animal's complete genomic and Total Herd Reporting data under the Pfizer logo on the Association's web portal. The much larger American Angus Association is still eating its heart out over that one.

It's unanimous. Everybody in the division wants her on board full-time perm. They've thought long and hard about where she'd best fit.

"I've enjoyed every moment," Laura says. "I don't want it to end either. But it's only fair to tell you I'm considering opportunities closer to home."

"Of course," deKoop says. "But let's continue. Once we've laid out a couple of possible career paths, Dr. Behrens will fill you in on the big picture."

The first option is marketing. Laura'd be an attractive, intelligent, highly presentable spokesperson who understands the breadth and depth and wide-ranging impact of livestock genomic assessment. She's perfectly attuned to their target audience. She'd ultimately be responsible for all media communications: television, webinars, YouTube, print and radio spots. She'd be the voice of the industry.

Or she could go into research. More upside potential, especially in the long run if she has management aspirations. Her thesis draft shows impressive technical skills and comprehension. She'd be eligible for tuition assistance if she decides to go on for a doctorate.

Since she's already signed an NDA, Dr. Behrens holds nothing back. He walks her through the division's roadmap for the next three years, a polished insider deep-dive she's sure he's done word for word to big investors. She has a once-in-a-lifetime opportunity to play a key role in Pfizer's secret effort to create a 50K test to measure and correlate fifty thousand distinct genetic markers for purebred Angus beef cattle. An order of magnitude more sophisticated than the Human Genome Project, where you can't openly discuss optimizing breeding for traits of economic interest. It will revolutionize animal husbandry, starting with seedstock producers like the Engebretsons.

Behrens is really pitching hard. He tells her there'll never be a better opening for someone fresh out of grad school. "Get ready for a rocket ride," he says.

They turn to her for questions and field them openly and frankly. They explain benefits and salary ranges.

It's only when the discussion turns to relocation that Laura expresses doubt. The company's mostly back east and scattered around the upper midwest. She's a cattlewoman with ties and obligations to a big family ranch. She asks about working remotely.

They tell her maybe in a few years. The lab's where she needs to be for now. Where all the action is.

Each of them closes by encouraging her to think it over.

She agrees to get back to them within a week or two. Hangs up and calls Branch. "We best talk. Can you get over here. Snow's slacked off some."

It takes him an hour. "Roads are bad," he says. "Real bad. All that wind-drifted snow on top of yesterday's glare ice. Can't see where it's slick. White-knuckled it all the way."

She's brewed up fresh coffee from some of the California beans he brought. Once Branch is halfway relaxed, Laura starts to jump right into The Discussion but she stalls out. "You mind looking at my plants," she says. "Tell me how they're doing, what they might need?"

"Sure," Branch says. "Curious to see how that device of yours is working out."

She leads him into the laundry room. Next to the stacked washer and dryer is a waist-high appliance the size of a small chest freezer. Laura opens the left door onto a dozen drip-fed marijuana seedlings under a fluorescent grow light. A clone dome rests on a shelf in back and a one-gallon pot in front holds a taller plant whose top and branches have been frequently cut back to create the clones.

Branch lifts a seedling out of the hydroponic tub. He inspects and feels the creamy white roots snaking out below hydroton grow rocks. "These look pretty good. No yellowing and they ain't slimy. 'Course they're young."

He inserts the grow pot carefully back where it belongs. "No sign of nutrient imbalance. Not so sure about the lighting though. Leaf development looks all right so far but your girls are already kind of stretchy. Doubt that fluorescent veg light puts out enough lumens, especially with that glass plate under it to contain the heat. Might try a 400 watt metal halide instead and watch for leaf burn. Either way move 'em to a bigger space soon as you can. And I'm thinking some of those girls are boys. Those real lanky ones."

"What I'm after," Laura says. "See if I can isolate a few males and clone off females from the best mom. Close-monitor the offspring for a year and I'll have records of everything there is to know about the sires, just the way we do it with cattle."

She opens the other door, revealing nine larger plants under a high-pressure sodium flowering light. Each plant bears a toe-tie label. Male branches close to flowering are loose-draped with baggies to capture the pollen.

"Still not much room in here. End of the day you won't get much yield."

"Who cares?" Laura says. "A seed factory's all it is. Every few months I can spin a new generation. For a cattle breeder that's a hell of a luxury. Couple of years, I bet I can backcross sires that throw consistent high-CBD progeny. Then we'll see how much longer it takes to isolate a line of homozygotes."

"Well," Branch says. "Got your own way of doing things, I'll say that. Rest of us, we're all about the best females. And boy did I ever luck out. With the plants too."

She doesn't care for the comparison or for being taken lightly. "Difference is you're growers, not breeders. I'm thinking herd. You're a crop at a time kind of guy."

"What herd would that be?"

"The one I see in my head. Spreads across Montucky, stops right at the border where the federales wait. Like a big Monet garden painting."

"Well, stay with it, Laura. You're doing fine so far. Just keep this puppy clean. Confined space like this, anything bad happens it'll happen fast and wipe you out. Bleach those tubs every time you change your nutes. Pain in the ass but it's part of the job. Bleach out the lines and drippers too."

"Household bleach?"

"Dilute it ten to one," Branch says. "Then run you a string mesh maybe three quarters of the way up toward those lights so the plants bend away or you tuck the branches back through. Keep you a nice level sea of green."

Back in the living room, both resting easy on the overstuffed couch, Laura figures it's time for the real conversation. She kisses on him some and then tells him about the job offer, watching him tense. "It's a lot of money," she says.

"How much?" Branch's voice is flat.

"They just talked ranges but I doubt they'd mention the high end if they weren't willing to go near there. Clearly wanted me to know they'll pay a premium to get me. Eighty-five'd be my guess if I take the research position. That's the one they really want me for. And they're not shy about the bonus word."

"Jesus, to start?"

"We could tear down and replace that old barn of yours before the year's out," she says.

"You know I—"

"I know you'll take your uncle's money and you'll take money from that snake Hampton, but you won't take money from me."

"Only if—"

"I know," Laura says. "Only if we're married. And you still don't get what a cruel position that puts me in. You know I'm—"

"Not ready. You've made that plenty clear."

"You could come with me, find something out there, just for a year or two."

"Kalamafuckingzoo? No I couldn't."

They've said these things so many times Branch's ringtone is a relief, the chorus from "Panama Red."

"Hey, Hamp," Branch says as soon as he IDs the number. "How's it going?"

Laura watches him listen and hears him say, "Sure, now's good." And then sees Branch stiffen.

"You've got to be shitting me," he says.

His face isn't giving away much but it can't be good news.

"Well, guess I can understand that."

He listens and then says, "So starting when?"

"Mighty dickish behavior if you ask me," Branch says. "I'll send you a final bill." He hangs up.

Laura looks a question at him.

"Change of plans. Hampton's going to have the California guys run the grow op. I'm out."

"Just like that?"

"Sound business decision, he says. They've got the expertise. Moves the schedule to the left. Says he's lucky to get them."

Laura pulls back and looks at him. "I don't believe this. All you've done for him, including introduce him to the guys he's shitcanning you for? Bring him back all that weed and you just roll over?"

"Do you care? I mean really? It's what you wanted. Don't pretend you're not glad."

"Got nothing to do with it. Can't treat you like that. Star 69 his ass, I'll tell him so now."

"Anybody don't want to work with me, end of story. You know I got my pride."

"Not even the respect to tell you in person. You know I don't use the word except invitationally, but fuck that son of a bitch. Might just drop in on wifey for a little woman-to-woman chat."

"Let it be, Laura. Please. Done's done. I should've listened to you all along. Knew what you were thinking but I believed what I wanted. Didn't see any way otherwise, get back on my feet 'fore the boom passes me by."

She just nods.

"Look at the bright side," he says. "At least now I don't have to move to Tightsqueeze."

"So instead we...?"

"Tough it out on my own. Grow as much as I can at the ranch. Keep delivering to places nobody serves."

"I said we. I'll help."

"What, send me money from Kalamazoo?"

"Help you here. Long as you're not with Hampton and you promise to keep it legal, I'll work by your side. Ranch gal to the rescue."

Doubt in his voice: "What about Pfizer?"

"Only if they'll accept something part-time, working from the Research Center here. They told me no but maybe if it's that or nothing. My advisor's already offered to let me keep using it, long as I share my findings and give them credit anytime I publish. The Association website gig's still mine if I want it, but they can't pay much. We'll figure something out."

Branch stares at her. He can't shift gears this fast. "I'm done thinking for the day. Can we not talk about plans or weed or DNA anymore?"

"Sure, honey. Let's get something to eat and just cozy up. There's always tomorrow. And I'm not ready to lose you. I'm scared of losing us."

"You said a mouthful. What do you feel like?"

She calls in a delivery order for a whitesauce pizza while Branch stokes the fire.

The snow outside stops. The wind dies down.

Laura opens a bottle of wine when the pizza arrives.

Once the dishes are put away they move to the couch and hold each other for an hour or so, just staring into the flames. They're mostly silent until Laura turns to him and says, "Fuck me silly." Invitationally.

# CHAPTER TWELVE

# PROVISIONING

"Can't just back your semi up to a loading dock," Johnny Legal says over late-night coffee in a Denny's he prefers for confidential meetings, "start dollying out pallets of equipment and fifty-five gallon drums of nutrients. Way too obvious. And sure don't want it delivered; paper trail could haunt us years from now, some RICO shit."

"So?" Brendan says.

"I'll drive the truck up. Friends in Oregon rented it there for local return. Said they'd be hauling antiques. It's already stashed down here. Lots of miles to pay for but nobody'll ever know who or what or where those miles went. You're the chase car. We'll have radios. You bring any smokables, make sure it's under an ounce and you got your card with you."

"When you want to go?" Brendan says.

"Be where I tell you Friday night. We'll roll out before dawn, blend in with the weekenders. I've got guys ferrying equipment from Chico in small delivery vans to where the truck's at. We've got a couple of resale cards on file there, clean businesses. All cash sales. We're doing this right."

When the time comes, Brendan drives Fast Horse east into the Gold Country foothills through Grass Valley and Nevada City and along a ridge high above the South Fork of the Yuba.

He always names his sponsor-leased macho rig Fast Horse. This year Fast Horse is a limo-length Lincoln mall-terrain vehicle called the Navigator L. It's three tons unloaded, dirge-black on 22 inch rims, with deep-tinted windows obscuring his personal possessions.

Brendan flips on an interior light and quickscans Johnny's directions, turns left at the Washington turnoff and descends into a deep gulch and past the little town's assay office, grocery and old hotel. Nobody is around to see him pass. Few house lights are on.

Once the road bridges the Yuba into the Tahoe National Forest it turns to dirt and darkness is complete, tall trees blocking out the stars.

A few miles further Brendan finds the right gate with the padlock hooked over. He locks it behind him and follows a gravel driveway down to the river and a rustic estate home of reclaimed redwood, roof festooned with solar panels. Majestic conifers shine golden warm, uplit by skylights and tall Pella windows.

Intruder lights come on. One of the garage doors opens. Brendan drives in and parks next to a 26-foot U-Haul Jumbo Hauler.

Johnny Legal leads him into a designer living room and offers him espresso.

"What's the story on this place?"

"Vacation rental," Johnny says. "People we know. Reserve it every fall, give them a percentage of what we trim, dry and bag up from back in the woods. All very cool. Way more private this time of year.

Nobody sees a thing. Don't want you to worry. You ready for adventure?"

"Ready for years."

# CHAPTER THIRTEEN

# TURNING PRO

For the next few summers, as soon as school was out, Branch and Brendan strode the trails of Montucky, Branch often moving up into the lead, growing stronger and toting more than his share. Around evening campfires they'd discuss Lewis and Clark, the expedition slave York and the Shoshone teenage bride, Sacagawea. Wondered aloud why Charbonneau of all people was her husband until Branch read that the French Canadian won her in payment for a gambling debt. They agreed that she could easily have had her choice of any better man in the Corps of Discovery. William Clark, in particular, was real sweet on her.

Back at the house they talked almost every day about the mountain men who came after the Journey of Discovery. Branch ordered library books and devoured them. Whenever Brendan drove them through a town large enough to have a bookstore, Branch tugged him over to the western history section and made him buy any book they didn't have. Branch read them all and then retold the stories to Brendan and Hattie. Where those men travelled. What they accomplished and how. Everything but why. Brendan and Branch didn't need to talk about why. They knew in their bones.

When Branch turned high school sophomore, Brendan's life took a turn too. Wrestling couldn't take his students very far. Unlike some parts of the country, it wasn't popular at school and no one watched but other wrestlers. Students who were good at it went out for football instead. Once out of college, there was no future except crude, phony wrassling on television. Mixed martial arts had a tiny cult following. With few rules, almost no states allowed it. No television network would show it.

But Vegas and California started changing all that. Like cocaine a few decades before, celebrities seemed to pave the way. Actors and musicians were seen in front-row seats beside beautiful women who wouldn't be caught dead at a boxing match. The extreme violence seemed to satisfy an unspoken need.

The public took notice. Dojos and gyms sprang up in larger cities. Cable television started airing cage matches. They were scary and exciting. People hated or loved them.

It started to look as if wrestlers might have a professional future after all. Brendan's college students asked would he coach MMA in the evenings if they paid him privately.

Brendan said he didn't know much about it but there was a gym over in Albuquerque that specialized in Asian and Brazilian combat sports mixed with traditional boxing and grappling. Told them he'd go down and see what he could find out.

After watching his first workout Brendan signed up for training and spent every weekend there for the next several months. He found that he loved it more than any other sport. It was like wrestling without restrictions. You didn't pin a guy. You choked him into unconsciousness or bent his limbs the wrong way so he tapped out before they shattered or popped. Or, standing, you beat and kicked him until the referee called a halt. It was primal. It was as real as being alone in the wilderness, alert to any attack. The only way to survive was to demolish.

He got good quick. He learned to strike, sparring with emerging fighters who came there to prepare for high-altitude matches where thin-air conditioning was crucial. He was hard to defend against and hard to prepare for. Nobody fought like him. His unusual body type, weird gait and rhythm, and the unrelenting ferocity of his attack earned him the nickname, "the Bear." He overpowered conventional fighters.

In 2001, the Bear fought his first professional MMA match for Japan's Pride organization when it was in its ascendancy. It was one of the first fights they televised for the U.S. market. Brendan dominated his opponent from the get-go, finally scoring a knockout with a looping overhand right.

A few months later Pride took a slide when their head honcho was found hanging by his neck. The media called it a face-saving suicide after his mistress left him, but few believed a Japanese man would kill himself over a Japanese woman. Those in the know hinted that Pride was a yakuza front that failed to honor its obligations.

Brendan's televised fight was replayed over and over and the world took notice. With Pride's decline, worldwide MMA focus shifted to the U.S. where it became the fastest growing sport. Television was soon saturated with unforgettable images, frantic announcers, hysterical audiences.

Brendan rode the wave with a string of victories to sold-out crowds against increasingly well-known opponents.

Then came the World Trade Center bombing and Operation Enduring Freedom. The public's warrior ethos and battle mentality grew to its all-time high since D-Day. The networks trumpeted the way these productions were being sent to the brave men and women defending our way of life overseas as the cameras cut to troops in desert camouflage screaming with youthful bloodthirsty abandon.

Times couldn't be better. Within a year Brendan was making enough money to hire a manager. He quit teaching so he could train full-time and take fights wherever they were offered.

He quit visiting Montucky too.

# CHAPTER FOURTEEN

# WING JOINT

Why'd you bring me here of all places?"

"Doubted you'd much care for the dorm," Branch said. First time he'd driven her downvalley from the church compound for a taste of his new college life.

"A beerjoint?" Hattie said.

"Sports bar. Something you need to see. Something I need you to see anyhow."

Widescreens on every wall showed silent tractor pulls and monster trucks. Athletes in various costumes disported themselves in all sorts of ways on every kind of field, track, course and court. Liquored-up guys glanced walleyed from one to the next when they weren't staring at her, just about the only woman in the Wing Joint.

Hattie forced her own eyes from a demolition derby to her menu. "You know I can't eat none of this."

"Not here for the chicken," Branch said. "I'll treat you to a real good salad someplace else once we watch this."

"Watch what?"

"You'll hate it."

Every widescreen suddenly switched to the same channel and flashed rapid montages of cartoonish fight scenes. Each knockout punch victim exploded into an animated skeleton.

The crowd noise exploded. "Turn it up!" shouted beer-laden voices around her.

Martial music and over-amplified voices in unison blared exaggerated low frequencies and reverberations Hattie associated with Satan's minions.

She panicked, reliving for the first time since high school the absolute terror of seeing old Dutch paintings of hell. Sounds and images raced through her head: crowds jeering inquisitions, gladiators; believers facing lions. Salem witch trials. Pandemonium.

Ordinary members of the Activity were allowed television sets if they watched only news and documentaries. But Hattie as a Keeper of the Flame had to abide by more stringent rules. She hadn't once looked at a television since the day she and a Texas jury gazed at one before acquitting her. Freed her to regain custody of her young son and flee to the sheltering arms of the Church Universal and Triumphant.

Twenty screens at once overpowered her. She felt a seizure coming on. "What is... Why did you—"

"Called a reality show," Branch said. "Some reality."

Fanfare from speakers and barroom noise subsided as images of Las Vegas traffic gave way to an establishing shot that swept across the elaborate grounds of an ornate sheetrock palace.

"What are you talking about?" Hattie said.

"Writers' Guild went on strike awhile back. Actors wouldn't cross the picket line. Networks couldn't film anything with a script. Either fill all that dead air with talking heads or jam supposedly real people into close quarters and stick cameras in their faces."

"Branch, I don't understand."

"Surprised everybody," he said. "Audiences really got into it, the weirder the gimmick the better."

A camouflage Humvee stretch limo circled an artificial waterfall and disgorged a horde of halfdressed thuggish men. Sporting odd combinations of hair, tattoos and piercings, they swaggered into a vast entryway.

"So here's what it's come to." Branch said as he clinked his beer against her waterglass. "These guys are all fighters. They share a house for months, practicing to maul each other."

But she's seeing peaceful, domestic scenes around the home. Meals together. Conversations in dorm-like bedrooms and lounges. Letter-writing.

"Some become friends. Some turn enemy. Tensions rise week after week. Big brawl at the end of each show, a lot of shouting as one guy eliminates another."

Hattie wasn't tracking his words. Her head throbbed. She gulped the rest of her water.

"Nice word, eliminate. Lose a fight, they send you away and we watch you react. Maybe you're still belligerent. Maybe you whimper'n whine. Or claim it's an opportunity, go home to your baby mama, learn from your mistakes, train like hell to work your way back up."

Branch waved a waiter over for refills.

Hattie shuddered at the silver eyebrow ring. But more, way more, at Branch. Where'd he get his cynicism? This familiarity with the devil's ways.

"Last one standing after thirteen weeks is the ultimate fighter. Gets a small check, big belt, short contract to go hurt some other guys next year."

Everybody onscreen marched out to poolside patio tables where they slugged down pitchers of beer. She couldn't make out the phrases they were tossing at each other, but the change in tone was unmistakable. Gangland jeers and taunts grew louder, fiercer. Stinkeyes glared.

Her own eyes felt as if they were on stalks, swiveling from onscreen beerspills to the cowboys and college boys sloshing beer around her.

Underneath her revulsion Branch saw fear. "You don't recognize him, do you?" he said. "Table all the way to the left? One sitting farthest from the pool?"

It's a shaveheaded pumped up burly guy with a Mephistopheles mustache and goatee. "Branch, how would I know any—"

"That's Brendan. Except they don't call him that. They call him Bear. They all got to have nicknames."

"Our Brendan? It can't be. Branch, are you sure?"

"Man I wanted to be just like growing up? Hell yes I'm sure. This cartoon bear."

Hattie put her hand over Branch's and started to say something reassuring, she didn't know what, something a mom would say while still reeling, just as the room around them got way more boisterous.

Hattie turned her head to see everyone staring at the monitors. Anticipation brought them to their feet.

A Hispanic-looking fighter at one table looked over at the one adjacent and said he couldn't wait to kick that guy's black ass.

The black guy said you don't have to wait.

Someone overturned a table and chairs flew everywhere as the two men went at it. The Wing Joint erupted.

Jabs and roundhouse rights and lefts led to a takedown. The men rolled around, fisted skulls bouncing off the concrete deck. Onlookers—nobody was still sitting—made way and stood clear. This wasn't a competition; it was anything goes. Kicks to the groin, knees and elbows to the head.

The defender got back to his feet, bleeding badly from nose and mouth. He body-lifted his opponent and jackhammered him headfirst into the poolside concrete over and over until blood stained the water pink.

The restaurant crowd made animal noises.

The victor tossed the gory mess aside and said straight into the camera, "Bleep called me out. What the bleep did he think I was gonna do? Deserves what he bleeping got."

The camera returned to the unconscious man and slow-zoomed in on his pulped head before pulling back to show the reactions of the other fighters. They righted their chairs and sat down to resume drinking. Except for the victim still unconscious and unattended in the background. Then the screens faded to black.

Followed by an ad for a testosterone supplement.

As the noise level in the Wing Joint died down, Branch realized that Hattie was chanting. Hard at it too, her pitch rising and tempo increasing with each repetition. He recognized the Violet Flame decree. Surprising himself, out of habit or love or empathy or because he hates what Brendan has become, he joined her.

*I AM the violet flame*
*In action in me now*
*I AM the violet flame*
*To Light alone I bow*
*I AM the violet flame*
*In mighty cosmic power*
*I AM the light of God*
*Shining every hour*
*I AM the violet flame*
*Blazing like a sun*

*I AM God's sacred power*
*Freeing every one.*

Their eyes locked, mother and son who had been through so much together whirled the verse faster and higher until the syllables merged in a trilling warble. Drinkers around them laughed, exclaimed and high-fived each other.

Hattie took Branch's hands and signaled with a squeeze the end of the chant. After a moment she said, "Why didn't Brendan do something? He could've stopped it."

"This reality's only got one rule," Branch said. "Don't never get in the way of the camera."

# CHAPTER FIFTEEN

# META TANTAY

Northeastern Nevada's mile-high mix of flat scrubland and craggy hillocks flash by on Brendan's left, broken by steep piñon pine-dotted foothills. Rugged mountains loom behind.

Across the highway the Humboldt River is low this time of year. Beyond, a long push-pull freight rolls toward the Carlin tunnel, three locomotives in front, one behind.

Brendan's been thinking about the sweat lodge a few miles to the north, as he does every time he passes by. Hasn't used it in years, since Rolling Thunder died. But this trip his memories seem way earlier.

Brendan thumbs the squawk button on the World War II suppressed-carrier single sideband radio telephone velcroed to Fast

Horse's center console. The ancient device is one of Johnny Legal's strategies: security through obscurity.

The signal is weak. Johnny, a quarter mile ahead in the U-Haul, is barely in range. Brendan speeds up to get closer.

Its frequency band was abandoned decades ago. No scanner can pick up a signal without a closely pre-matched receiving frequency, Johnny told him before they left. Wouldn't hear voices anyway. Even so, tradecraft prevails: only short, innocuous messages.

"Dude, we gotta talk," Brendan says. "Next exit pull into the Pilot station, okay?"

At the Carlin exit a small sign announces they've arrived "Where the Train Stops... and the Gold Rush Begins."

Brendan hopes the gold rush part is true.

They park in the gas station and he slides into the U-Haul's passenger seat. "Change of plans, Johnny. I need to pull off for the night. You go on to Elko, twenty miles up the road. Good place to stay is the old Star Hotel right on the main drag, used to be a whorehouse. Basque restaurant next door. Steak and lamb are good. I'll meet you there for breakfast."

At first the guy is incredulous. "No way. I don't drive without chase car protection. And I don't stop for the night at places I don't know."

"The place is fine. We're way out of any danger zone. I need sleep and a good sweat."

"How you're gonna sweat? It's cold out here."

"Sweat lodge I used to come to awhile back after a fight. Recuperate and shift gears, get ready for what's next. Need that now more than ever. Big changes, man, and I'm in considerable pain."

"When'd you last get a good night's sleep?" Johnny says.

"Early this week sometime."

"Told you let me hire some moving guys. Shouldn't have packed all that stuff yourself. Hampton'd've paid for it."

"Not used to people doing for me."

"How heavy you into those painkillers?" says Johnny Legal.

"Not much. Half dose at a time. Any more I couldn't drive this tired."

"You got my alarm bells ringing. Being sent off somewhere alone all of a sudden smells like a setup."

"You're kidding, right? Something happened to you, way worse'd happen to me."

"Lawyers don't kid about shit like this."

"I'm not sending you anywhere, Johnny. Stay wherever you want. Call my cell in the morning, tell me where to meet you. This ain't about you."

"Hell it's not. Give me your keys and you take the truck."

"Where I'm going it'd stick out like a flying saucer."

"Fuck you. I hate this. We can't screw it up, Brendan. Ain't like I'm hauling a little product. They'd stack so many federal felonies on me. You knew that before we left."

Brendan flares. "I'm done arguing about this. It's a done deal. Hit the road."

"I made a big mistake asking you to drive with me. Thought I could trust you. You'll never put me in a position like this again."

"My loss."

"Draw me a map where you're going to be. I run into trouble, I hand it over and they round you up within the hour. Otherwise I'll see you at breakfast. But early so I'm not so obvious. Anything changes I'll text you. If you don't have cell coverage out in the sagebrush, call me soon as you hit the highway. I don't hear from you, all bets are off."

# CHAPTER SIXTEEN

# WHAT NOW

Laura and Branch relax into their new agreement. But they back away nervously each time one sidles near to talking about what it is they've agreed to.

She calls deKoop, thanks him for the opportunity but says she's got local commitments that preclude her working for Pfizer full-time, at least for now. She wants to keep working *with* them, though. Could she come visit once school's out to discuss how they can stay teamed up with her representing the Tumbling E and the Angus Association? He reluctantly agrees but says he hopes continuing to work together will convince her a closer relationship is in her best interests.

She talks to the Animal Science faculty about maybe doing some postgrad independent study work so she can keep using the lab and other facilities. They agree if she will credit them in anything she publishes and give Montucky State University first crack at publishing her longer works. Starting with her thesis, which her committee has just approved without requesting any changes.

Except for wrapping up her coursework she's done with her degree earlier than expected and her future options are pretty open. She starts to slowly contemplate them.

With Hampton out of the picture, Branch is now free to replan for his future and theirs.

They tiptoe around each other, trading what-now glances.

Eventually Branch, to his credit, mans up. Over breakfast at his place after a great night together, he says, "What do you think you'll do with your condo? Maybe lease it out?"

Laura keeps her voice level. "Why would I do anything with it? Where would I live? How would I get to the research lab?"

"Well, I thought here. With me. Save us some money."

She sighs and shakes her head. "Hey please, Branch, believe me, I'm not taking anything away from what you've done here. But I could never explain moving out here to my folks. They invested so much in my education. They believe in me. They love me. Expect great things from me. And they'll do anything in their power to help me get wherever I decide I'm destined."

"And that can't be here, with me?"

"They'd be heartbroke if I turn my back on the Tumbling E. Us carving out a meager existence here, they wouldn't get that at all. See it as rejection, rebellion. I'm a big part of the ranch and it's a big part of me. They're as excited about the genomic work I'm doing as I am and we're all eager to get together and discuss how best to apply it. These are exciting times for seedstock producers."

"So what, move back in with Mommy and Daddy?"

"No. I don't see living there. I'm a researcher, a brain worker, not a ranch hand. Maybe someday if we decide ranch life is for us, I suppose we'd go talk to them. They'd offer up whatever's the most suitable spread they've got and all the support in the world. We'd live comfortably among friends and family."

"Huh. Until then you're fine with us living in our two places, seeing each other now and then?"

"We'd have more time together, here and at my place. And your work'd have four hands instead of two."

"That's future enough for you?"

"I need the academic community. I need lab access for whatever I decide to do remotely with Pfizer. And something you'd find out about me is I'd get cabin fever so bad cooped up here through a winter. It wouldn't be pretty and I'll guarantee you wouldn't like me very much by February or so."

"So, same old limited commitment."

"Damn it, Branch, don't you get it? We're both in transition. We can grow side by side. Why draw some line in the sand now?"

"Guess you and I are different that way," Branch says. "I know what we've got. I know what we can have together. I don't want to wait and say maybe or keep asking when. Be sure you're right; then go ahead. I'm sure. Why can't you be? It's all hesitation with you."

"Listen, bucko. Don't paint this as me being too weak to decide. I am the deciding one. I've thrown in with you. It's you who's hesitant to explore except to grow weed. You want to lock us into something fixed and rigid, and you want it right now. There's a real conservative streak in you I don't much care for. It's not your best quality. I told you I'd help you. But I never said that's all I'll be doing. Now that school's out you're going to see how ambitious I really am. I have the inside track on staggering changes in the whole livestock industry. I'm for sure going to make my mark. So we best be helping each other."

"Feels like your family and me are gonna be rivals and I'll be the one out on the fringe."

"Only if you want to be. Don't think you've been around extended family much 'less that church was it. If you and I are together, everybody'll take to you and take you in."

"What about the weed? Last Thanksgiving I didn't get the sense they'd be too into that."

"It's a conservative community. True they don't look with much favor on their kids turning into stoners, running off to Portland. And that whole gateway thing. They hate hard drugs and anybody peddling 'em."

"See, though, I believe in what I'm doing as much as you do your work. Hard to be shy about it. I tell people about what medical cannabis did for me, my injuries and operations. How it helped my mom. I know not to evangelize but, back me into a corner and ask me about it, I'll generally speak my mind."

"Just be discreet. Give discussions like that some time. To them you're a builder. No reason they'd associate you with marijuana. They won't fuss much about you and me. Like we say back there, love me, love my dog."

"Well, hell, doesn't that makes me feel special? So what now?"

"I'll visit home once school's out. Spend maybe a week, do some serious family planning."

"Now you're talking."

"Family business planning, smartass. Maybe you could come out for a couple of days when we celebrate their anniversary. I got a nice gift can come from the both of us and you'll have a great time, see how we do a big old-fashioned whoop-de-do."

Branch just sighs.

"Deal?" Laura says.

"Deal," Branch says, though not perhaps in as strong a voice as she'd like. He was going to have to grow into it.

Their handshake turns into a good bit more.

# CHAPTER SEVENTEEN

# LEAVING PARADISE

Branch was barely getting by doing remodels and repairs, weekends and off hours, for a Hyalite general contractor named Sullivan. But how was he going to finish his second semester, already down to just fifty dollars and payday a week away?

Had to hold out was all. Month or so, he'd start logging overtime hours 'count of spring's longer days. Make it to June, he'd have fulltime work. Enough to pay tuition next year.

But when he arrived at the office one mid-March Saturday to clock in and get his assignment, old man Sullivan called him into his office. "Close the door," he said.

It's bad, Branch thought. Was he being laid off? Anybody had to go he'd be the one, the new kid and part-timer to boot. Did somebody complain about him? Or, worst of all, was something missing from a job site and they suspected him?

"Have a seat," Sullivan said. And then just gazed at him.

Branch didn't know what to make of the look. He said, "I know I've got a lot to learn yet, sir. I've never been part of a, you know, formal construction crew. But I'm a hard worker. I really need this job."

"Relax. I'm not firing you if that's what you think. Other way around. You familiar with what's going on over to Big Sky?"

"The ski resort for rich folks? Some. It's down near where I'm from."

"I doubted it'd take off the way it has," Sullivan said. "The first condos in the public section at the bottom of the hill were pretty crappy. But the guy who started the gated Yellowstone Club up top? He's took it to a whole 'nother level. Million dollar ante to become a member. Huge annual dues. Two mil to buy a ski-in lot, bare land. Five mil and up for a condo. Six mil and up—way up—for a residence."

"Dream on," said Branch.

"Hey, people are signing up. Rich out-of-staters wanting a peaceful family place for a visit and a charter jet to pick 'em up and bring 'em back. Private helicopter shuttles from the airport."

"Who has that kind of money? Why would they come here?"

"Celebrities. Bill Gates. That vice president, the stupid one, forget his name. People got places all over the world but most aren't private getaways where they can pretend they're ordinary folks and never see any. Former U.S. bicycle champion, that Tour de whatever guy, invested and became their spokesman. Ten thousand foot perfectly groomed mountain. Sixty ski runs. Multiple golf courses. World-class restaurants and lodges. Full-on concierge services. Catered hand and foot. Point is, they're paying it. Place is successful. Big land boom going on. Construction boom."

"Something in it for you?"

"Not sure yet. Local architects and interior designers are getting big reputations doing elegant rustic. But it's harder for builders. Site challenges and weather challenges. Just the cost. But years back I built a couple of hideaways for east coast guys like to fly fish. Stone and logs, open beams with antler chandeliers, pools and saunas and such. Coordinated with their architects so they trust me. They're asking am I interested in building and flipping spec homes."

Branch said, "Seems like a lot of risk. Go over budget, something that large, who eats the loss?"

"These guys build city shopping centers. They're used to big numbers per square foot. Something the size of these houses, four or five million to build it out, one house at a time, I can leave a huge margin of safety. And they're offering me a percentage after it sells. A couple of successful projects could set me up to retire."

"Well, look, Mr. Sullivan, this is all way out of my league. I'm just a college kid. Any way I can help, count me in."

"Hoping you'd say that. I'll be paying wages, but for the first house they'll be about what I'm paying now. In your case that's not much because you're new. But everybody likes having you on the team. You learn quick and you're steady. But you'd have to live down there."

"No problem with that if it can wait till school's out. I could work weekends until then."

"I'll tell you straight, kid. If I've got any openings this summer I'll hire you on a temp basis, sure. But everybody and his brother's a laborer come then. I want you right away. You see how much I'm ready to commit. I need big commitments from my men. At 7500 feet elevation the building season is way short. We need to be closed in as much as possible before the snow falls. We're only a couple of signatures away from starting site prep. You're young and single. You live in a dorm. What's holding you back."

"My mom will take it hard if I drop out of school my first year."

"Talk to your instructors. See what they can do. Or take incompletes and finish up in the dead of next winter. You can always go back to school when you're flush. Who else you know your age or with your experience gets a chance like this? Construction's boom or bust around here and it's been real slow for a long time. I was you I wouldn't hesitate. Think of the satisfaction, working on one house at a time you can be proud of, start to finish. It's a bumpy business, Branch. Be a fool to turn this down."

Branch didn't go back to school. He got a bonus when the first house sold. Sullivan bumped him up and gave him a small equity stake in the second.

The Yellowstone Club boom raged on just the way Sullivan predicted. Builders, craftsmen and providers of luxury goods were making extraordinary money for Montucky. While other desirable areas of the state drew waves of outlander financiers, software and media executives, none compared to the Yellowstone Club.

Branch saved enough to invest directly with Sullivan on their next two spec houses. After that, Sullivan retired and cashed in his chips.

Branch set out on his own, backed by the same investors. He lived on the cheap; neither he nor his mom had much in the way of personal expenses. He rolled his profits from one project to the next, relying on subs to build increasingly luxurious homes rather than hiring large crews. With his track record, banks were willing to give him construction loans or finance land purchases.

Then everything started to fall apart. The economy tanked again. The Yellowstone Club flirted with bankruptcy. The cyclist got into a bitter, very public controversy blowing the whistle on performance doctors doping other cyclists, including the American cycling hero who succeeded him. The Yellowstone Club advocate was on the right side of the scandal but the headlines were devastating. They made a mockery of the clean outdoor family image the club was touting. Members started withdrawing.

Another PR blow fell when the cyclist was seriously wounded by a hunting companion's "sound shot" at something he heard but didn't see. The shooting didn't happen in Montucky but it reinforced perceptions of the club as a refuge for rich urban dwellers pretending a couple of weeks out of the year to be outdoor enthusiasts. Toxic lead buckshot lodged in the spokesman's heart, further damaging the club's reputation.

More lawsuits followed. A pilot was fired after telling a reporter other club pilots flew prospects in while drunk or drugged. And then the Environmental Protection Agency obtained a $1.8 million settlement for illegally dumped materials after ski runs were bulldozed without a permit.

Members resigned and put their homes on the market at way below cost. There were few takers. Facilities were closed or abandoned before completion. One remaining member owned a hedge fund and teamed with a prominent Swiss bank to help the club continue operations and pay off its existing debts with a new loan so massive it could never be repaid. Flush with money from this "loan-to-own" scam—more bad publicity—the founders divorced, took the money and ran. The cyclist investor and his family used the Swiss bank's valuation to sue the club for millions. Still more newspaper stories.

Worst hit was the cottage industry of local builders, plumbers, cabinetmakers, decorators and other tradespeople. Bills went unpaid. Only lawyers prospered.

Contractors who hired subcontractors were particularly devastated. Once his current project, a five-bedroom chalet, was framed out, Branch laid off his subs and short-term hired a retired carpenter and cabinetmaker friend if he needed help. He negotiated with his savings and loan association for extensions.

Working later in the season than he should, he fell from an ice-slick scaffold. His injuries required several surgeries and a slow recovery. He developed a prescription painkiller dependency.

And then Hattie fell ill. It turned out to be breast cancer, metastasized before being discovered. She had a mastectomy and radiation therapy and chemotherapy. What she didn't have was insurance.

Branch kept working on the chalet as long as he could afford and sold it to another builder for a modest profit if he didn't count his labor. Once the construction loan was paid off, most of his remaining money went to buy a small rundown ranch outside of Pony that had been on the market for years. It needed a lot of work to be a working spread and nobody would loan on it, so he low-balled an offer. He figured sweat equity was about all he had going for him.

He and Hattie moved in. He hired a dour, middle-aged widow named Vanderkaden as live-in caregiver and cook.

Montucky passed a medical marijuana law. Branch got a card for Hattie and one for himself. He set out to make the place more livable and learn to grow cannabis, hoping it would ease his pain and Hattie's nausea. Hoped he could wean himself from prescription meds.

As Hattie's condition worsened, Branch did something he thought he'd never do. He tried to call Brendan.

His phone calls got routed from one person to the next until he finally got through to a guy named Natty Gason who said he was the Bear's manager. Branch explained who he was but the guy wouldn't divulge Brendan's number. "Give me the message and I'll pass it on to him," he said.

"It's personal."

"The Bear don't take personal calls from guys don't have his number."

"That's why I'm asking for it. It's a family matter. It's important."

"I've known the Bear a long time. Don't recall him ever mentioning a nephew."

"We haven't spoken in years. He ever tell you he used to come up to Montucky a lot?"

"Think I recollect something like that."

"That was my mom and me when I was a kid."

"Tell you what. Give me your number."

Branch did.

"I'll tell the Bear. He wants to call you he will."

Branch got hot. "This isn't some damn crank call and I won't be screened. Give me Brendan's phone number or I guarantee he'll be mightily pissed."

After a pause the manager yielded. Branch dialed immediately but the call went straight to voicemail.

"Uncle Brendan, this is Branch. First off, I apologize for dropping out of touch the way I did for so long. But you were like a hero to me and I… I couldn't stand what you were turning into, this whole celebrity fighter thing. I was kid enough to need you still be you. Anyway, I gotta talk to you. We need you to come up here, least for a day or so. Ma's dying."

# CHAPTER EIGHTEEN

# TRAIL

Brendan Glass, thirty-six going on two hundred, guides Fast Horse north along a rough two-lane and then cuts east on a dirt track into what years ago was the intentional community Meta Tantay. Now it's an arid collection of collapsed lean-tos, yurts, willow benders and dilapidated canned ham trailers amid weed-ridden garden plots with fallen fences. He steers past the remains of a riverrock bathhouse abandoned only a few courses up.

Time to find out if who or what he suspects is inside him is really there. Rolling Thunder saw its presence, just the way he carried early shamans around inside himself for guidance.

Brendan dismounts and breaks out his hatchet and survival gear. Hundreds of boulders form a spoked medicine wheel that leads down a clay ravine to a turtle petroform above a meager artesian spring. The stone turtle shape surrounds a deep firepit filled with scorched sauna-like stones not far from a wikiup of canvas-covered latticed willow saplings and treebark. Two buckets and a big metal dipper hang on hooks from a cedar post.

He dips water into one bucket, gathers brush and then chops wood he pyramids over the rocks, shaving off a few flakes of magnesium from his firestarter to spark with his flint and steel. The hatchetwork loosens him up some but the pain that's been growing in him since the trip started is no less.

He tends the fire until the blaze mounts skyward. He breaks out another corncob pipe, loads it with bud and sparks it with a small firebrand. He smokes a bowl, knocks out the dottle, smokes another.

This late in the year the artesian spring is just a seep. He takes off his shirt, scoops a hollow in the dirt nearby, pisses into it and smears the mud on his arms and chest.

He continues stoking the fire and waits for the stones to heat.

Sitting close to the flames in a yoga position, he closes his eyes and tries to meditate his way into a trance state. Put the road behind him and work on his head. Sublimate the pain and get ready for what's to come.

When the heat gets too intense, he uses one bucket to scoop out glowing stones and carry them into the sweat lodge where he drops them into the empty firepit.

Back outside he ladles more water from the spring into the other bucket and carries it into the wikiup. He strips and lies down experimentally. The sweat lodge smells, well, inhabited. Musky. Then again, so does he.

He pours water onto the rocks. Steam billows. The sweats start.

Rolling Thunder always said it clear. To pass through injury or illness you have to choose when to confront it. Study up on what's ailing you and make your stand. Embrace it no matter what it is.

Brendan medicates for all he's worth, not to dull the hurting but to intensify and confront it.

From memory or maybe from right here in this sweat lodge, Rolling Thunder's voice says, "You ready for this, son? Let yourself go. It's winner take all and devil take the hindmost."

"Bring it," says Brendan Glass. He adds some hot stones to the pile, throws on more water. Abandons himself completely. Dives deep into the painpool.

He's gone for a long time. Doesn't know how long. Could be hours; could be years. Feels more like a century or so.

He regains consciousness in a dreamworld, jolting through a forest on a makeshift litter. The fresh scent of pines is strong. Brittle autumn needles from overhanging branches brush against him and fall on his upturned face.

He sees only vague shapes through narrow, swollen slits. Strapped down, he can't tell who's carrying him.

His body is ripped apart. Agony he's never known.

And he's really old. He's in shock. Did he Rip Van Winkle away years of his life?

His mind drifts away from the jarring ride through the woods. Dwells on Hattie's belief in reincarnation. Branch's insistence that, growing up, the Brendan he knew was a genuine mountain man, not a city creature fighting made-up battles for others' entertainment.

Some weird genetic memory inhabits him. He's thought for years he was different that way.

Or maybe something stronger. An old mountain man, say. Strong enough to try to take him on now and take him over. Maybe the end of his fight career loosened his grip on an identity he's taken for granted. Maybe fight injuries weakened his body and spirit enough to leave this presence an opening. Or what Natty did to his blood.

Brendan's lost enough fights to know when an opponent senses his weakness and moves in for the kill. And, just as in his losses, as the adversary draws closer his warrior sense can see and feel it much better.

It all makes a weird sort of sense. Old Hugh Glass is in there, suffering the wounds of the bear attack. The old guy's experience got imprinted on him somehow. Or in him.

Maybe Hattie was right: Previous lives aren't uncommon, just misunderstood. No point in thinking about it anymore. He's way past reasons and explanations. It's all about now. Whenever now is.

Rolling Thunder told him what he had to do and he's not done yet. Brendan Glass lets go of Brendan completely and dives straight into the old man's pain.

Old Glass remembers the start of the fight. Knew he was in for it soon as the silvertip grizzly didn't drop from his only rifleshot. Reared up huge instead, lunged and let loose that first mighty swipe.

No chance to reload so Glass unsheathed his knife and stabbed where and when he could as she ripped and chawed him apart.

No memory once he passed out till he was jerked awake by fingers pulling on his throatskin so others could whipstitch torn flaps together.

Now old Hugh Glass is lying on rocky ground. Can't see much or hardly move but hears a creek nearby to his left and pine pitch popping in a campfire to his right. He can smell the woodsmoke and can't miss the sound of voices arguing there. It takes a few minutes before he's sure the shrill, uncertain one is Jim Bridger, the teenager some call Jamie, a decent kid.

The other, deeper, might could be that troublemaker, John Fitzgerald, complaining that he's tired of waiting for the old man to die. Every day increases the chances an Aricaree scouting party tracks them down. "What's the point? You know he's going to die anyways."

Bridger says, "Ain't sure he's ready to kick off just yet. Gonna wash him up again, change his bandages."

"Waste of time," the older man says. "Infections'll take him. Bandage cloth'll have more use back at the fort."

Glass likes this conversation not at all but wants to hear more. He feigns unconsciousness as moccasins whisper over pine needles coming his way.

Mountain men rarely wash. Someone else washing him is new. He flinches when a wet rag touches the bad wounds, especially the ones on his back when he's rolled over. He flinches too when he's rinsed where only he's ever done, or a whore, after.

Finally he feels a coarse blanket thrown over him and his head lifted. Lips taste water he can't sip or swallow. Some runs down his throat anyway. His shallow exhalations bubble it out his near-demolished gullet to roll down his chest.

He loses consciousness. When he comes to, the voices are arguing harder. The deeper voice says, "You ain't taking that bear paw. What makes you think it belongs to you?"

"Putting it in his belt pouch. Belongs to him, not you or me."

"Aren't you the sentimental fool? We ain't leaving his shite behind. Pack up his knife and his possibles bag. I've got his gun. Time to go."

"Can't leave him unarmed." Bridger's voice grows more shrill.

"God damn you for the insolent pup you are. We don't take back his weapons, we can't prove he's dead. We don't get the eighty dollars. Don't know why as you're here but I ain't sticking around for my health. Or his."

"Man needs his rifle and his knife."

"Needs 'em where? You some sort of Indian? Think he'll use 'em in the happy hunting ground?"

"Suppose he lives—"

"S'pose he don't. S'pose you keep jawin' at me. Might find he's contagious. You could catch what he's got and I'll just tell ol' Henry the

Rees got you on the way back. Say I buried you too. Mebbe he'll pay twice as much for double the graves."

All old Glass hears after that is some shoveling. He's rolled into a shallow depression and then footsteps fade away until only the soothing sounds of the creek next to him are left.

He wakes up, passes out from the pain, wakes up again.

Finally he can distinguish light from dark. Then he starts to regain some control over his body, starting with his eyelids. He can see blurry tree outlines.

Eventually he's able to move the fingers of the arm that ain't broke past the stitches holding a flap of scalp on. He reaches over to cup his hand in the creek and scoop it back to his dry mouth.

A day or two later hunger starts to pang him—a good sign even if he can't do a thing about it just yet. But hunger cuts both ways. Come twilight he makes out a pair of wolf cubs bellying toward him. When they get about yea close he clenches his one good fist and practices a small growl of his own. Throat feels as if it might hold. Be bad if he reopened the wound with a shout and gushed blood from his neck. No wolf'd resist that.

The whelps back off. Their next approach, they tug the blanket off him and slink away out of sight, but not so far he can't hear them chewing on it. With luck they won't come back after him until tomorrow night.

Be nice could he build a fire.

Come dawn old Glass claws his way out of the shallow grave. The arm that's not broken drags him toward a sarvisberry bush nearby, bone ends grating in the leg that trails behind.

He fingers a few berries off the branch. Chokes them down but passes out from throat pain and exertion. Revives feeling a tad better. Thinking for the first time he might make it.

Long days follow. Hugh Glass binds two fairly straight deadfall branches onto his leg with a strip of blanket left behind. He mourns the loss of knife and especially his rifle, but he'd never be able to carry it anyway.

One day he feels strong enough to start crawling downstream. Raw bloody fingers of one arm and raw bloody toes of the opposite leg do all the work. One eye does all the seeing.

Can't kneel, much less stand, so he gets by on ground-level roots, berries and bushbark. But the she-bear inside him demands meat.

It's nothing but dumb luck: One day he creeps up on a torpid bulge-bellied rattlesnake stretched across the trail asleep in the sun.

He brains it with a rock. Removes the straight razor from next to the giant grizzly paw in his belt pouch. Slices off the head. Buries it for safety before flensing and chopping the reptile into small bites that he chokes down raw, wetted in the stream so they slide past his healing throat wounds.

Two days further down the trail he runs across pocket gopher holes. Unstringing the rawhide from one moccasin, he fashions a snare over the freshest hole and waits.

Waits some more.

Best gopher ever.

Meat makes him stronger but his back stinks and he feels flesh sloughing off. Be ugly, die of gangrene, all he's been through.

Heard tell of an old Pawnee trick so he drags his carcass to a rotting log. With great effort he rolls over so his back arches across it.

A few stitches he didn't know were there stretch and tear before he feels beetles and maggots creep in to work his dead flesh.

A few days later he fancies he's smelling better. Hunts up a grassy spot near a shallow pool and flips over onto his back—easier to do now—and shakes out insects and larvae. Flops into the pool, washing out anything loose in there.

Crawls to the bank. Reaching back best he can, he packs himself with creek mud to keep out the flies.

A week farther downstream he smells something other'n himself. Fresh kill.

Follows the tracks of a small bison herd. Comes across a small pack of wolves feasting on a dead calf.

They stand taller than he does so he waits until they're sated. He crawls up and scares them a few feet away before he looks for any good parts left.

The wolves hang their heads low, growling, before they head out.

Old Glass lies there a couple of days choking down as much as he can until the meat gets too rank.

He feels strong enough now to get to his feet. Spots a lightningstrike cottonwood and dulls his razor carving rude crutches from its branches. Finally pulls himself up to where he can lean against a tree. No more crawling for him. His arm and leg have knitted up some. He practices putting weight on them.

A few days later he's crutching along okay when he comes across an Indian camp, just now abandoned by the look of it except for three scrawny dogs tended by an old woman.

She gives him a long look he can't interpret before hobbling off to the edge of the clearing. The dogs follow but eye him as he gathers up some twigs and sifts through the campfire ashes for live embers.

Uses his razor to chip off flakes of flint from rocks just up the slope and then spark the tinder.

Once a small fire is going he drags back some dry wood and feeds the flames.

It takes longer than he expects to coax the first dog to his outstretched palm.

Clubs it to death with his crutch and roasts up a haunch.

The old woman appears nervous. He tries to sign to her that he means her no harm but she limps on down the game trail. Hugh tosses entrails toward the remaining dogs so they don't follow her.

Next day he pitches meat ever closer to the fire, drawing in the second dog. Day after that, the third.

He dries leftovers to take with him, gathers and pounds some berries and mixes everything into pemmican for the trail. Mostly should be downhill from here to the Grand, where he figures to fashion a raft to float him downriver to the Missouri.

Play it by ear from there. Retrieve his knife and his gun.

Getting-even notions devil him some but they're hard to hold onto. Stealing from a dying man is bad behavior, sure, but revenge is a wearying emotion 'less it's a matter of life and death.

Confronting those rascals will be fun. Watch their faces change once they lay eyes on him. See who he is now, by God. Hear what he's got to say.

# CHAPTER NINETEEN

# HIP STRIP

Natty Christ, formerly Natty Gason, pokes at his Polycom conference phone, silencing the goodbyes, his downlines reinvigorated for another week. He stands, stretches, slings a backpack over one shoulder and threads his way through xCeed cartons and packing tape scattered across his Duckburg apartment floor.

Locking the door behind him, he strolls out onto the Hip Strip, a bounce in his walk, a new man in a new land. But shaving his head might've been premature. A storm is blowing in. He tugs his watchcap lower.

The Higgins Street bridge takes him over floe-dotted Clark Fork waters. Natty leans into a headwind down Main Street past a string of headshops he browsed yesterday, asking where's the best place to buy medicinal weed. The consensus was the refurbished office building just ahead.

Once inside, though, the setup is weird, a long empty hallway of doors without signs or other evidence of habitation.

At the end of the corridor a handwritten paper taped to the grid-reinforced window cautions him to wait to be buzzed in. It takes a minute or so.

He enters a featureless reception area furnished with an empty desk beyond protective glass. Not a jar of product to be seen. An overhead security camera winks at him.

Finally a woman in her twenties comes in empty-handed, a mixed message of tie-dyed blouse and severely pulled back hair. She speaks into a bank teller's microphone. "Can I help you?" Sounding not at all as if she plans to.

"Like to see what you've got available, maybe make a little purchase. Got a California card, understand it's legal here in Montucky."

"Maybe so, maybe not. Does you no good here. We only serve our own patients."

"Well, don't you see, that's what I'm getting at. I've moved here and need some help to set up as a Montucky resident, find the right caregiver. Heard you're the best in town. Thinking my Cali card'd be enough to try a sample or two at least, confirm you're right for me. I've got hemis. Crohn's Disease. My medical records all right here in my backpack."

"We require a recommendation from a Montucky-licensed doctor."

"Can you help me get one of those? I don't know my way around yet; want to do the right thing."

"I'm afraid we can't accommodate you."

"Not even to get a doctor? So I can become your patient?"

"I'm sorry. Sir," she adds, with some finality.

"At least tell me where I might locate a doctor who'll recommend?"

"Few are accepting new patients. One down the Bitterroot in Victor. A lady up in Whitefish."

Natty matches her tone. "Might you share contact info?"

"One thing we're not, sir, is an information service. You'll have to inquire elsewhere."

"Point me, please. One of those elsewheres."

She gives him a look: Will you leave me alone if I do?

Natty waits.

"Try kitty-corner across the street. They might be more, um, accommodating."

Natty says, "Is it true you offer a strain called Paranoia?"

She buzzes him out.

Back on the street Natty takes a deep breath of fresh air and readjusts his wool cap. So far so good. Place is ripe for the taking. In a California dispensary she'd've had him Skyped up with a tame doctor and the form half-filled out by now.

It takes him a minute to figure out where she meant. Maybe the small building looks like a converted gas station.

Approaching the storefront Natty sees, yes, this is the place. Small sign on the door, Totally Hydro Concepts. Big initial caps to make sure you don't miss the reference.

Inside, there's no resemblance to the last place. Natty scopes out the mismatched chairs near the door where college kids wait facing a couple of desks sporting edibles and jars of weed. A raggedy customer is leaning over with his nose deep in a tilted jar. "Mmm. Nicer'n yesterday's. Let me have a quarter of that?"

"If I've got that much," says the caregiver behind the desk, midtwenties in plaid and denim, maybe a grad student or back after a stint in the service, straight-looking except for the little soul patch in his chincleft. He empties the buds onto one tray of an Ohaus triple-beam and weighs it out. "Little over a gram light. How about say you take the last of it, I only charge you seventy? Or sixty-seven fifty."

The customer digs into a jean pocket for crumpled bills the caregiver smooths out and slips into a desk drawer.

Place is as casual as the other was uptight. Kind of a barber shop vibe with everybody looking on to check out the other guy's action. No one's paying Natty the least bit of attention, a dude nobody's ever seen before. This is more like it. He sprawls out his feet.

The patient steps over Natty's legs, stuffing a ziploc into his jacket pocket. "See you tomorrow," he says back over his shoulder. "Maybe later today. 'S a game on."

"Catch you then."

Like kids playing musical chairs, everyone stands up, moves down one, takes a new seat and waits.

When it's Natty's turn the guy behind the desk says, "Hi. Don't think we've met. They call me Fast Eddie." He reaches across the table with a straight handshake.

"Hi, Eddie. I'm Nat. Or call me Natty. Just moved here. Don't have a Montucky card yet, like to get started. I've got mine from California. I'm told rules here say you can honor it?"

"That we can, that we can. Could I see the card please?"

Natty digs through his wallet. "Got two." He hands them to Fast Eddie. "One's the kind we actually use down there; each clinic prints its own. This other's the official one I think you want. Issued by the county, authorized by the state. Got it just before I left so I can be legal here."

Fast Eddie holds it to the light and flips through a thin binder with xeroxes of different state cards. "First one of these I've seen," Eddie says. "Looks real." He shuts the binder, hands the card back. "Thanks. Unusual name, you don't mind me saying so."

"More unusual than usual."

"Okay, Nathaniel, you're cleared for takeoff. Fact is you're better off than we are. Your card means any caregiver here can sell to you. In-state patients just got the provider they signed up for. I'd like to earn your business, be that one. So what's your ailment? Whaddaya look for in your medicine?"

"I've got Crohn's. And hemorrhoids. Miles and miles of piles. Pain and digestive problems. And I like to get really high. A sativa or sativa blend? Anything along those lines?"

"Some really good Jack Herer around. Spendy but worth it."

"I like it fresh, in good shape."

"Don't we all."

"Just mean I'll pay extra for da kine."

Another jar comes out of a desk drawer. Natty does his best connoisseur act, eyeballing and sniffing. Expresses the right amount of admiration. "How much of this can I buy?"

Eddie gives the jar an appraising eye. "You're allowed an ounce, which is more than I got today. Suggest you buy a little, say an eighth, see how you like it, come back tomorrow I'll have more. Or try something else."

"An eighth now wouldn't count against the ounce limit tomorrow?"

"Law's silent about how often. An ounce at a time is all." Eddie leans back. "But we're getting ahead of ourselves here. Talk to a lawyer if you want fine interpretations. Way I roll, soon as I think you're buying more'n you can use yourself, you're eighty-sixed for good. No second chance. Life's too short."

"Fair enough," Natty says. "But I like to do a lot so I hope you're kind of flexible. Don't want to use too much of your time; you got people waiting. Tell you what. How 'bout you sell me say half a dozen different strains you think I might like, you got that many, eighth of an ounce each. Label 'em so I know what's what and I'll A-B 'em at home, see what's right for me, come back in the morning to provision up. That work for you? What time you open up?"

# CHAPTER TWENTY

# NEW BACK

Dogmeat and dogjerky ain't more'n a memory as Hugh Glass follows the old woman's tracks. Not just hunger has him hollowed out. Something bad's going on deep within his back. Ain't healing the way it should. Smarting something fierce.

He catches up with her just as she rejoins her people, a small band of Dakota Sioux camping anywhere they run across bison or antelope. It's not a war party so their leader signs to him that he's safe. They know of him for his battles with their sworn enemies, the Aricarees.

They minister to his injuries. He hears gasps as they turn him around and peer into gaping wounds near his spine where the grizzly scooped out backmeat to sling to her cubs. Pockets of infection glow cherry red. The Indians make wriggling finger motions to describe little worms inside.

Once he's cleaned out they apply potions and lotions concocted from roots and shrubs. For distraction he watches two women brush a fresh elkhide clean, measure it to his back and trim it.

A tribal elder signs for him to lie face-down. The rough-hewn face says this will hurt.

The pain of the first sinew stitches knocks Glass out.

He wakes to a dying fire. Tries to shrug but his shoulders don't get far. He has a new back, sewed on to protect the angry flesh inside.

The Sioux break camp, leaving him jerky enough to recuperate before resuming his trek.

Soon he's making pretty good time swinging along on his crutches. He follows the Grand to its confluence with the Missouri and finds a couple of *voyageurs* repairing a bullboat seam with pine pitch. Once they get over his appearance they give him a ride downriver to Fort Kiowa, 350 miles from where he started.

He arrives early in the evening and hammers on the stockade gate. Two soldiers catch him under the arms as he sags. They drag him into a messhall filled with men who believed Fitzgerald's account of Hugh Glass's death and burial. In the flickering light they see a ghost.

Might be funny but the two fellows Hugh's looking for are gone. The handcrafted skinning knife James Bowie sold him a decade before in an Under-the-Hill Natchez saloon is on its way to Fort Henry on Jim Bridger's belt. And John Fitzgerald, part of an expeditionary force heading up the Yellowstone, still has Glass's rifle.

A combat medic applies whiteman medicine to his wounds and changes his bandages. The army paymaster ponies up back pay for provisions and new clothes. The old mountain man's ready to head out.

It's November. Every day counts. Too late in the year for boats journeying up the Missouri where he needs to go, so Glass takes the next boat heading downriver toward the mouth of the Cheyenne or even the

North Platte. Extra miles afoot but he'll maybe have a clear trail west before the plunge north into icy drifted realms.

# CHAPTER TWENTY-ONE

# PONY

"Don't schedule no more fights for a while," Brendan told Natty. "I need a couple of months off." He didn't mention the phone call from Branch. Just said he needed to regroup.

Once back in Montucky, Brendan's life on the ranch settled into an easy routine. He didn't dare break training, but a high-altitude poverty-stricken ranch offered plenty of strength training and cardio. Tons of heavy old things to lift and to toss. Stumps to uproot to clear new pasture. Boulders to wheelbarrow and wall off fields. A sunken corner of the barn to jack up for a new foundation. Concrete to mix and to shovel.

Mostly he liked to run. Take off after a cup of daybreak coffee down the twisty road skirting Hollowtop. Then charge full speed up game trails. Traverse the big talus slope under the peak, knees high to lift his feet free of scree, hips swiveling to keep his balance. Then angle down to the Crevice and Strawberry lodes and past the ten stamp mill a couple of miles into Pony. From there back home down the road above North Willow Creek.

Branch was still recuperating from his building accident so Brendan ran alone. After lunch, though, they'd work together fixing up the house. Branch had a contractor's ability to plan. Brendan had the strength of many and liked working for him. They enjoyed great conversations, making up for the years they'd missed.

One evening at dinner a couple of weeks after Brendan's arrival, Branch brought up those years.

"Don't care to talk about it," Brendan said.

"I was young. I'd built you up to be—"

"And I got real busy."

Hattie put a whatever look on her face, looked toward the sky and whistled a few notes. "Clouding up outside. Think we might get rain?" she said from under her chemo cap.

Everybody relaxed.

"Heard you got married," Hattie said.

"For a while," Brendan said. "Didn't take. Just the once for you, Hattie?"

"Should be an easy answer but it ain't. Anyway, all the men I loved are dead and gone except the two of you here. I'm fast getting there myself. Where's your ex-wife at now?"

"Back in the stacks, I guess. Still the college librarian where we met, last word I got. We don't speak much, just birthdays and such."

"What happened?" Branch said.

"Young college professionals, had no money, me assistant coaching and her with her library science, we thought we knew who we were and what we wanted and more or less how we'd get there. Promotions, maybe tenure, have a few kids. Couldn't've been more wrong if we'd been trying."

"You started martial arts after you split up?" Branch said.

"Other way around," said Brendan. "Schoolkids talked me into it. I didn't know dick. Sorry," he said, looking over at the widow Vanderkaden, who never talked at dinner unless asking someone to pass the food. As far as Brendan could tell she never smiled—certainly not at him—and she shot him a look now that let him know coarse speech was yet another thing about him she didn't like.

"We wanted to stop renting, buy a little house, so Christie finally agreed to me working weekends as a sparring partner, bring in a few extra bucks, maybe turn pro. Didn't neither of us see any further'n that."

Hattie said, "Branch showed me some of that fighting dirty on TV. I can't believe you'd get mixed up in something like that."

"Wasn't what we planned."

"How'd you get to be so mean, hurting people for a living?" Hattie said. "You were the sweetest, gentlest kid I knew back when we were close."

"Money, mostly, at least at first. Became a TV goldmine. MMA fans'd watch the same match twenty, thirty times. No other sport has those kind of numbers. And then pay per view took off. Promoters could pull in tens of millions at the gate, but PPV could easily match it. It cost next to nothing extra. But they needed fighters who'd live up to the hype, put on a show, deliver the goods, go for fight of the night. Damn few of us could live up to the billing. Happened I was one."

"And your teaching?" said Hattie.

"Had it up to here. Same with Christie's librarianing, I'm afraid. Sick of it all. Didn't want to think about it. Didn't want to hear about it."

Branch said, "How 'bout who you'd always been? Didn't you care?"

"Turns out there's a fighter in me," Brendan said. "Always has been. I just didn't know it until then. Face an opponent across the cage and it surges up inside. Kill or be killed."

"So you were really into it?" Branch said. "For a long time I thought—I hoped—you were just role-playing."

"No way," Brendan said. "Realer'n anything I've ever done."

Branch gave him a curious look but said no more.

After dinner they adjourned to the living room to medicate with some fine NorCal sungrown Brendan had brought up. All but the widow Vanderkaden, who abstained. "Never tried the demon weed. Enjoy my whiskey though of an evening."

The marijuana helped all three of them, but Hattie the most. Cancer was eating her and the chemo was eating her; until now the only thing not eating was her. But her old self started to reappear and her good mood was returning.

"Let me guess," she said. "Your Christie didn't like this ferocious warrior as much as the guy she married.

"She tried," Brendan said. "Give her that. Came to my first few pro fights. But the injuries and the brutality; it was all too much for a gentle girl like her. Hated all the lowlifes and the hype. Just like you, Branch. Can't blame either of you. So we settled for me buying Christie the house we'd been saving up for and I moved down to Albuquerque to train full time."

"And since you split up?" Hattie said. "A string of fierce women in your life?"

"Hard to find your soulmate in a gym. Ladies there see fighters just another exercise machine."

"None at all?"

"Thought back on one from my past but our lives had gone in real different directions. Didn't see how it could work out."

"Missed opportunities," Hattie said. "Well, maybe in the next life."

Brendan said, "Long as we're getting so personal, something I don't know how to ask."

"Can't speak for Branch," Hattie said. "But if it's me you're talking about, ask me anything. Better you get your answer now'n next month or next week."

Brendan said, "Branch and you are so matter-of-fact about what's happening to you. Talk like it's just another milestone. Seems like neither one of you's angry or scared."

"Not death that worries me," Hattie said. "Dying don't scare a believer. We've all died and been reborn so many times it's old news to us. Karma's what we care about. Whether we're working our way toward Ascension or backsliding."

"You've done nothing but good," Branch told her. "You'll be reborn even better."

"Got to be hard for you to watch, though," Brendan said to Branch. "It sure is for me."

"'Cause you see body death as the enemy," Branch said.

Brendan didn't know what to say. Of course it is.

"Branch had to deal with his daddy's passing early on," Hattie said. "Made him wise beyond his years."

"Not one to preach," Branch said. "But there's comfort to be had in pondering reembodiment and rebirth. Might help."

"Tell you one thing I didn't expect," Hattie said. "Closer you get to this life's end, the more your old ones come back to you. Dreams and sometimes just looking out at the view. More pleasure in it than you might think. Branch, how about you help Mrs. Vanderkaden in the kitchen? I'm tired but I need a word or two with Brendan before I turn in."

They were alone. Hattie patted the space next to her on the sofa. Brendan joined her.

"Remember when we was young?" she said.

"Think about it every day I've been back."

"Me too. Glad we had the chance before everything changed. Funny, isn't it? Those breasts you admired so much, and didn't I too, God knows? Loved to look at myself in the mirror. One gone now in a specimen jar or for all I know a landfill. The other not much to look at. They helped bring us together and here we still are."

"They was perfect," Brendan said. "And you're still great as ever."

"Make you a deal," Hattie said. "After... this runs its course, we ever find ourselves in the same place at the same time, let's not wait for nothing."

# CHAPTER TWENTY-TWO

# KNIFE

When Glass steps aboard the pirogue in the morning he's surprised to see the Québécois trapper, Toussaint Charbonneau. Man's terrified of boats and water. What's he doing here?

Frenchy's the worst interpreter Hugh knows but he's been doing it since before Lewis and Clark. Burly, swarthy, fleshy, he still bears some remnants of a hatchetfaced youth: dark eyes, bushy mustache, a weird chinbeard no wider than his nose.

It's not just water Charbonneau's afraid of. He's afeared of everything except his half-dozen Indian wives so far. Bought 'em young and beat 'em often, the only fighting he's known for. Hides at the hint of trouble.

But cowards can outlive heroes. Frenchy's childbride Sacagawea, far stronger, is long dead. Word has it their son Pomp's in some German castle getting a classical education paid for by Clark, a captain now.

Old Glass takes a seat athwart Charbonneau and drops his rawhide-bound blanket roll, everything he owns inside. "Been awhile," he says.

Charbonneau looks him up and down. Says, "Can't say the years are treating you well, Hugh."

"This one less so than most. Where you headed, Frenchy?"

"Meet up with Black Moccasin, the Minitaree second chief, you know him? Asked me to help parleyvoo with Hudson Bay Company traders down this way to talk pelts. Required to shut down their fur factories so they aim to set up a big rendezvous every spring. Trading post without the post; everybody brings what they got to sell or barter. But ol' Black Moc wants the company to come to him first soon as winter breaks 'cause he's northernmost up on the Knife. Figures his tribe should get a better price with just one trader buying it all and not so far for them to haul back the plews. I'll be the old man's *négociateur*. How many years, him? Must be eighty by now. Join up with us for a few days, Hugh. Won't likely see Indians get that old no more."

"Can't do it, Frenchy. Paying my passage hunting up grub."

Charbonneau says, "Owe yourself a good time, don't you? All I hear you been through lately. Black Moc's got him a peace pipe tall as he is, dresses up in these fancy duds, berry-dyed quills from *le porc-épic*, beads all over his slippers. Still does the Dog Dance better'n most and purely loves to pass that peace pipe around. I need someone to pass it on to or it comes back sooner'n I'm ready for, him all feathered up and puffing like *la cheminée*. You need you some relaxing, Hugh. Don't have to be setting out this time of year. Stick around a few days and then stroll back downriver to Fort Kiowa with me when we're done. Get healed up there for the winter. Go where you're headed come spring."

"Ain't in the cards, Frenchy. Henry's building a small fort up by Three Forks and I got a score to settle."

"Don't doubt that, you being somewhat less dead than reported. Be a cold damn walk though, as little meat as you got on your bones. Freeze out there all alone. How you going to stay warm and fed with just what you got in that blanket roll?"

"Get my rifle and Bowie back I'll be good as any other galoot. Compared to what I had getting this far I feel rich, even with just a loose-handled knife and this here cheap smoothbore. Got me flint and steel in my shot pouch again and that's enough fixins to make a man feel right pert."

"Well then," Charbonneau says, "Guess long's neither your string nor mine runs out, we'll meet up again next year."

Once the old interpreter disembarks the next morning there's more room on the boat.

Several days later, as they're nearing the mouth of the Laramie in late afternoon, Glass goes ashore again to hunt. He ascends a broad bluff a quarter mile to the east that parallels the river. It's easier going than the brushy riverbank. Better visibility and nothing in the way when he shoots.

He limps north, upwind, scanning for game grazing below or headed for water.

Whoa. Rifle fire ahead. A lot at first before it tapers off.

He gets to where the noise is coming from but now it's mostly whoops. He sneaks to the edge of a rock promontory with scrub pine behind to mask his silhouette. Flops to his belly. Watches Aricarees drag the pirogue up onto the bank, pile crew bodies on top and try to set it ablaze.

The boat is too wet to do much more than smoke but the Indians gather enough cottonwood branches to make a pyre.

Tough to watch but staring at death ain't nothing new.

He's startled by a shout from down below. Some sharpeyed bastard's spotted him.

Glass starts running east across the mesa but it's a mighty poor effort with his leg. Can only hope it'll take the hostiles long enough to crest the bluff that he can go to ground. Must be someplace he can lurk till nightfall. Then he might can skulk away. Maybe get down to the Laramie and find him a hidey-hole.

Ain't much but featureless dirt and parched buffalo grass up here though. Nothing to hide behind. No hint of a sheltering declivity or coulee to crouch in.

He's still looking when he hears a birdcall from down below, answered from somewhere up here where he's at.

Old Glass spins around with his weapon. Scans fast and tight, twice, before he sees a small Ree hunting party coming at him from the north.

He turns toward the southeast but no way can he outrun them.

Worse yet, he hears hoofbeats and sees an Indian pony coming straight at him from the east. But his old eyes still work okay. Rider don't look Ree. No gun or bow showing. No club or spear raised for the easy kill.

Hell, he knows the guy. Young Buffalo Teeth, the Mandan who used to guide him hunting.

Twice decimated by smallpox epidemics, the Mandans are trading post Indians these days, tight as ticks with trappers since before Lewis and Clark came through. Their villages hug forts for protection and barter goods. Aricarees on the warpath call them weak, but the Rees outnumber Mandans ten to one and have more guns.

Glass doesn't flinch as the rider bears down on him at full gallop.

An arm reaches down. Glass grabs it and is swung aboard. Smooth and easy as can be but stitches pop and backskin tears.

Both men laugh, racing across the mesa. The Rees shrink behind.

An hour later he's being doctored in a Mandan prairie lodge. Women joke with each other as they pack his wounds with God knows what and menfolk pass the pipe around, retelling his rescue over and over, the story getting coarser each time.

The pipe comes his way again. As soon as he passes it along, the women roll him onto his belly and stitch his back up.

A few days of Mandan hospitality is enough. Glass figures by now the Rees have given up looking for him. He sets off overland with a small iron kettle rolled up in a sougan strapped on his back—gifts from the Mandans to replace some of what he'd lost in the boat fire. And, of course, his smoothbore, knife and his possibles.

It's late November when he points his way northwest to bisect the great arc of the Missouri and come out at its headwaters.

Ain't easy miles. Early snowstorms are a blessing and a curse. They drive elk and deer down from higher elevations so by mid-November there's game aplenty. But no time to skin it out and make jerky with winter coming on so hard and fast. He needs to keep moving.

Keeping warm's a challenge. Compared to what he's been through, though, a spell of weather don't concern him overmuch. Reminds him he's still alive.

Never once sees sign of men as he forges a path through snow, hailstones, high winds and graupel. The Indians are in their winter camps and Henry's men should be busy, putting up the new fort where he's bound.

Except when old Hugh finally stumbles onto the Three Forks confluence of the Gallatin, the Madison and the Jefferson, he finds the new fort drifted up to the sills, abandoned half-built. No sign of hostilities. Just too cold and weather-prone to endure.

Where would they have headed? Snow's so deep it'll be hell trying to cut their trail.

Could've gone north back down the Missouri a ways looking for a more sheltered location, but they wouldn't get far before the valley narrows and cuts through steep cliffs. East or west would take 'em into mountains. That leaves the three headwater valleys to the south. But which?

Glass decides to play it safe. He holes up in the abandoned fort and replenishes himself with easy-to-track rabbits and such until a Chinook blows through and melts the snow down to where he might see sign. He packs up and does a concentric sweep spiraling outwards, looking for busted off tree branches or sign of campfires or hasty burials.

He's surprised to discover that they went east, back the way they must've come. Fled the Three Forks because of the weather only to head straight toward where it would get worse before it got better. What's the sense in that?

There's a whole string of towering north-south mountain ranges to cross before they could make winter camp on the lower elevations of the Yellowstone. Leave Sacagawea Peak behind and cross Bozeman Pass if they could find it in whiteout conditions. Else struggle across the mountains through storm winds from the west. Rest up before the challenge of surmounting the Gallatins. Then gird up for the two-mile-high Absarokas obscured by sideways blizzard gales strong enough to snowblind. No way to know if you're climbing or descending. No notion of what's a foot in front of you. If anything.

Survive that and, if you're not lost, skirt south of the Crazies and drop down to the Yellowstone with its well-worn trails to the Missouri and its settlements.

Couldn't've been much fun, nor likely to be when he follows. But if they could do it he sure as hell can too.

Six weeks later the old mountain man, feeling kind of spry, strolls into a rough-hewn expedition camp on the Big Horn to eyeball shocked trapper faces. It's Ghost of Glass all over again. Half the men think the bear did him in. The rest heard the Aricaree boat ambush got him last fall.

He's genial, no longer in a hurry. Takes coffee with the men, adding as much grog as they'll allow. Relates his recent travels and adventures, staying clear of any talk about the bear or the men who'd abandoned him.

Then he makes a beeline for Jamie Bridger, who's been refusing to meet his eye the whole time, sitting as far away as possible.

Bridger sees him coming and starts to bolt, but sinks back onto the bench, trembling. Appears resigned to his fate.

Hell, he's still just a kid. But a tough one until now. Old Glass politely requests his knife back.

The boy stammers out an apology.

Glass just gives him a look and says, "Shouldn't take things ain't yours. Folks might still need 'em."

"Yes, sir," Bridger whispers.

"Got me? Won't do nothing like that again?"

"Yes sir," Bridger says. "I mean no sir." He fumbles the sheath off his belt and hands over the Bowie.

"You're young yet," Glass says. He examines the knife carefully for damage.

"Yes, sir."

"Appears you took good care of 'er."

"Did my best, sir."

"Might have you some future if you repent your mistakes."

"I do, sir."

"Then you've nothing to fear from me. For your youth I forgive you. Word of advice though?"

"Sir?"

"Never touch a man's knife. Nor his dick."

"Yes, sir. Of course, sir. Just washing off the blood and bear slobber dripped down. Didn't think you'd want it on you and feared infection. You was unconscious, I thought, wouldn't know or mind. No more to it than that, sir. I'm too much the other way."

Old Glass straps the sheath to his belt, already thinking ahead. Fitzgerald won't be so easy. He's no kid and inclined to be disagreeable.

By now, Hugh's heard, the rascal's miles away with a small group that left the fort two weeks ago for the trading post on the Missouri, toting winter-thick plews.

Come morning, provisioned up, Glass is right back on the trail.

# CHAPTER TWENTY-THREE

# BEEFALO

Old ways die hard and it's still rude in Montucky to just up and ask a stranger what he does for a living. Might suggest a snap judgment of his personal worth. Truer in places where macro real estate fluctuations and spotted owl timber industry shutdowns don't change your life.

Come November, underemployment don't seem like a bad word. An unheated indoor job promising lots of exercise don't look so bad. Soon you're pulling green chain. Lumber mill boot camp; if you can't pull green chain you won't get a chance to do anything else there. It's pure hell at first and dangerous too. But once you know how, it's a long day but not a bad day. It's all about technique. Using your legs rather than your back. Requires speed and stamina and of course strength and agility. But technique is really the key. Because if you don't sort that lumber fast enough, you could be leaving fingers everywhere.

So you don't confront someone and ask outright. People want you to know they'll volunteer it.

But, other hand, if you're at a rip-roaring outdoor anniversary party where everybody knows everybody except the guy you're curious about, and he's the boyfriend of your host and hostess's daughter and you're her cousin, the guy's for sure fair game. You just ask someone else instead.

A strapping cowboy in his twenties ambles over to where Branch is refilling his plate. They howdy and shake. "Laura's cousin Ambrose," says the cowboy. "I've got a place just up the road. She mentioned you're a builder?"

"Construction contractor, yeah."

"What sort of things you build?"

"Residential construction. When times was fat I built luxury spec homes down in Big Sky."

"Money in that?"

"Sure was for a while. Then it wasn't. And I got injured with no worker's comp because I took the independent waiver. So I'm down to redoing an old ranch out by Pony by my lonesome."

Ambrose makes a show of scanning the horizon. "Pretty as this?"

It's a beautiful, crisp day at the Tumbling E. Fifty or so folks of all ages are gathered down by the creek behind Engebretson ranch headquarters on some of the nicest pastureland Branch has ever laid eyes on. The mighty Pioneer Range is just far enough away to be the perfect backdrop.

"Not even close," says Branch.

Laura's dad, Verle, is helping his small country/bluegrass band set up on a weathered outdoor stage: small amps and drumkit, a couple of old microphones and a pair of wobbly PA speakers. Verle's vintage fat-body Gibson archtop, a banjo and a button accordion rest on instrument cases.

Much of the crowd clusters around picnic tables laden with a vast assemblage of potluck dishes, or stands near beer kegs donated by the local distributor. Others move from group to group, carrying paper plates, talking loud and laughing louder. Men and women closest to the stage are already razzing the band.

An array of good-smelling Angus steaks and burgers—no surprise there—sizzle over hardwood chips and coals in a split-and-folded 55-gallon drum encrusted with years of sooty juices.

"How many acres?"

"Just twenty."

"All told, everybody put together, we got about ten."

Branch stares at Ambrose.

"Oh, sorry," Ambrose says. "You said acres. I was thinking sections. Much of your land arable?"

"Six, maybe seven acres. If that."

"Good soil?"

"Not at my place 'less you like to grow bricks. Was an old brickyard."

Ambrose gives Branch's shoulder a friendly slap. "Just funnin' you. Laura said you're up by Pony and I've Saturday-nighted the Pony Bar a time or two. Got to admit we're prouder'n we have a right to be of what we got here, considering the family come by it long before any of us was born. But, day like this, hard not to brag. How often you get to pull the leg of a guy from Pony?"

"Got every right to crow. Ain't ancestors keeping everything up so. Guess it means I can't much interest you in a land swap."

The band starts tuning to the squeezebox.

Ambrose says, "Tell you what, I don't know as you're a better rancher'n me but you're sure as hell a braver one."

"Can't really call it a ranch; I just don't know what else to call it. Falling-down fixer nobody wanted. Keeps my tools from rusting is all. I'm going to get a good seat over by where the music is. Nice meetin' you."

"Likewise," Ambrose says. "See ya'."

The band kicks off with Jimmie Rodgers' "Waiting for a Train." They play it relaxed and it turns out Verle can sing. His yodeling's right on the money too.

Laura comes over, her work in the kitchen done for a while. She puts her arm around him and he feels right at home.

Then she coaxes him to dance and he doesn't feel that way anymore. But he hobbles and flails and a lot of good-natured hooting and hollering is directed at them both.

Laura's been here all week so that evening they have to drive back in separate rigs. It's not until they're in her University District condo that Branch has a chance to say, "So?"

"First things first," she says. "Did you have a good time?"

"Wow, yeah."

"D'ya like my friends? Like my family?"

"Maybe not as much as they like you. They treat you like some kind of princess or queen. But sure, yeah."

"Treat you okay?"

"Treated me great."

"Didn't I tell you?"

"Just like you said."

"Next time I say not to worry about being accepted by someone I swear by, you going to trust me? Take me at my word? Do what I say? Not get your back up?"

"Much as I can."

"Good. 'Cause it's already next time. Lot to tell you and I need you to back my play."

"Family planning went all right then?"

"I'm so stoked. You'll like it if you let yourself. White wine or red? Would be champagne if I had some."

"Your choice, long as it's not sweet." Branch kicks off his boots. Fresh socks today so he puts his feet up on the coffee table and waits. Trying not to look anxious.

She returns with a Snake River Valley Tempranillo, tortilla chips from a local craft bakery and avocado dip. "You get much of a chance to talk to my brother Sid?"

"Yeah, a time or two. Just shooting the breeze. Nothing in particular."

"What'd you think?"

"Of him? Big and bluff. Seems real straightforward. Confident. Sounds as if he's kind of the Tumbling E operations guy, coordinates everybody. Guides all the families."

"Right. My dad Verle's still involved on the strategy side and makes the big business decisions, but he delegated the day-to-day years ago. Sid's done a tremendous job. Smart and good with people."

"People sure seem to like him."

"Plenty of loyalty both ways. But..."

"But?"

"Sid being the oldest, he's pretty much done what he set out to. Rather stop supervising, hand it off, go off in some direction of his own devising. Been hinting at that in emails since not long after I started grad school. Ambrose, being the younger, he's impatient to move up. With Sid guiding him at first and pinch-hitting if necessary, Ambrose can do the job just fine. Both got business degrees and everybody keeps everybody informed of what they're doing.

"I'd assumed our first family council business meeting together would be about me. But Sid stole the show. He described the transition real low-key like it was a done deal. Ambrose chimed in about his ambitions, his qualifications, how all he wanted was to keep the successes coming

"Everybody went for it. We all like continuity. Still need to bring it before the other Tumbling E stakeholders, extended family, but it'll fly. What everybody was wondering, though, was what's Sid planning for himself. And I'm curious about me. Sid and I are hand in glove in all breeding decisions and cowherd data management. Might be something in it for me?

"Sid told us, 'Tumbling E's big enough we need to diversify. We're near carrying capacity and we got all our eggs in one basket. Families keep growing. More people depending on us all the time. Too much risk for the likes of me.

"'Don't see anything on the horizon going wrong but something's always lurking. Ranching, every season there's plenty outside our control. Like what if mad cow disease shows up in Montucky or in Alberta again like ten years ago and a few cohorts from the same herd got shipped down here. Panic because one cow is all it takes. One dimwit guy in one dairy cow slaughterhouse wants to save feed money so his machine scrapes away at some poor old downer dairy cow can't stand up again. Guy figures what are the chances, hasn't been any mad cow in a decade, so he makes bone meal out of its brains, spinal cord, ganglia, intestines, eyes, tonsils, whatever. Feeds his other animals what no grazing animal should ever eat.

"'Even though we embargoed Alberta beef in less than 24 hours, it wasn't soon enough to keep the Japanese from embargoing ours, or the rest of the world jumping off the bandwagon. Sixty-four countries before it's over. Three billion dollar beef slump lasts eight years because how do you convince overseas buyers there's no risk. Hard to prove a negative, no matter what you tell 'em about range-fed, organic, finished off with our own hay, no animal byproducts ever, no bone meal ever, no chemicals, no food ever come out of a bag. And can't say's I blame 'em. Symptoms are slow to reveal so it can spread through a herd before anybody notices. Say you're a health guy or an ag guy, some heavily populated country? You lift the embargo and one day you see zombie citizens staggering down the street with terminal brain rot? That's a pretty big oops. Business school they call it a CLM. Career-limiting move for sure.

"'So how do we prepare for something like that? Like I said, diversify. But hell, beef is all we really know. It's what we're set up for.'"

"I thought Sid was doing okay. Not rushing it but holding everybody's interest.

"'I come into this,' he told us, 'openminded but with a few show-stopper criteria. Have to leverage everything we've done here and especially what we do better'n anybody else. Has to be a new chapter in the Tumbling E legacy, not a departure. Two: has to smack of some growing trend. Diversification again: traditional beef consumption is falling off. Three: needs a big barrier to competition, a moat. Four: has to stay Montucky, even if it goes worldwide. Five: needs the potential to go worldwide if we get ambitious.'

"I asked him, 'And the answer is?'

"'Beefalo,' he said. 'That's the opportunity. All kinds of reasons.'

"'Take diversification. No dependence at all on export trade decisions. Official USDA Beefalo Beef isn't distributed nationally in this country, much less internationally. Hell, it isn't even distributed regionally. You can maybe buy a burger online from one or two ranches, and if you live in Seattle there's a local route to restaurants and like that. But otherwise nobody ships, so if you want beefalo you're SOL. No way it's going to come to you.

"'Need you a quarter or a half or a fully dressed carcass? You got only two choices. You drive to someone's processing facility, wherever in the country it is, and toss your purchase in the back of the truck. Haul ass all the way back home before it turns bad. Butcher it yourself or have someone local do it. Or you pay more to the rancher to haul it to his meat market and cut it up. But then you're paying retail prices rather than hanging weight and you still got to drive all the way there and throw all those wrapped cuts in coolers in the back of your truck and haul ass back home before it turns bad. How lame is that? If we get an operation going, any size at all, be child's play to line up a distributor same as bison meat has.

"'Course most of the beefalo outfits are mom-and-pop operations with random-mixed progenitors, so they probably sell everything direct right at the ranch or at farmers' markets, to neighbors, through their local butcher shop, maybe to a local restaurant or two. So distribution's not a priority for them same way competition from them isn't a consideration for us.'

"Sid took us through Beefalo 101. 3/8 bison, 5/8 cattle of any breed or mix.

"'Some people claim the meat, properly raised and prepared,' he said, 'has the potential to outclass any other domesticated meat for flavor, protein, and health benefits. When grass-fed, rangy and lean but not gamy. Cooks faster and shrinks less so you can charge more per pound. Bison and beefalo aren't marbled like traditional beef. The fat content you need for tenderness is intramuscular and doesn't cook off. So you got to pull it from the heat sooner. 'Course restaurants don't mind that.

"'Trend we want to cash in on is healthier beef. Market it as the beef that's good for you. The other red meat. Less cholesterol and bad fats, anything you don't want, than skinless roast chicken, beef or even fresh cod. Appeal to the demographic that loves good beef but worries about what it might be doing to their hearts and arteries.

"'Every carcass trait our Angus EPDs measure comes out better than either the beef or the bison they sprang from. Guess we chalk that up to hybrid vigor, but it hints that the predictions and measurements we do so well with Angus will certainly be trickier with beefalo. But if we make that our challenge from the beginning it'll become a moat that we're smart enough to cross but anyone who takes a run at us'll lag behind. Our immediate challenge is to pioneer beefalo genetics and optimize the progeny with each generation. If we're good, our beefalo beef will be better and a key product differentiator from other proteins.

"'Beefalo also stand out in many of the traits of economic interest we've bred into our Angus herd. Easy birthing, small calves, fast growth, early maturation. Gentle and easy. Thrive on free-range grazing with hay in the winter. Unlike Angus, where grain-finishing increases marbling, beefalo can be grass-fed right up to the slaughterhouse door.'

"Then Sid dove into marketing. A small Association with an active Northwestern chapter to leverage. Beefalo Beef is an official USDA roll-stamped beef grade, like Choice or Prime. Little serious competition with hodgepodge lineages. It's like going to the dog pound. It's even kind of the same on the bison side. Cattle DNA has been intermixing with bison for at least a hundred years. Testing shows only four purebred bison herds in the western hemisphere, most confined to state or national parks, unavailable for breeding or purchase.

"'Once intermixing occurs, no breed-specific EPD measurements have predictive value, which seems to rob us of tools we rely on. But Laura's not so sure. Cross-species interbreeding experience is all anecdotal. She's looking into it. So far, beefalo history is seat-of-the-pants. Even what the beefalo folks call purebred means only it has roughly the right ratio of mystery buffalo and mystery cattle.

"'Long story short,' Sid told us, 'I think we can revolutionize the beefalo industry with our Angus cowherd and carve a slice out of the beef industry. We can trademark Angus Beefalo.

"'Then I started wondering how to introduce some predictability into the bison side. I pitched Laura with some vague research questions and she pointed me in a useful direction. The Yellowstone herd is the biggest collection of cattle-free bison stock and it's overflowing the park, with ranchers worried about contaminating their own livestock with brucellosis or just getting their fences trampled and winter forage gobbled up. So mostly the bison that come out of the park into Montucky are killed by park people who can't kill anything inside the park. Nobody much cares for that solution. Hunters wouldn't mind the bison being killed if they could be the ones hunting 'em. Ranchers want 'em killed anytime they get near private land and don't care who does the killing. Animal rights people don't want 'em killed at all.

"'And Indians just want 'em back. Last few years the Assiniboines struck a deal to move a couple of hundred purebred bison up from Yellowstone to the Fort Peck reservation near Poplar. Started out with 2100 acres but now they're up to 13,000 acres, which they think can support a thousand head, with some going to the Fort Belknap reservation.

"'Dad and I are in early-stage negotiations with them for breeding rights. So far it looks sort of promising. They're cash-starved but the bison are their heritage and they're only open to the possibility of dealing directly with serious, experienced ranchers who won't do anything disruptive or disrespectful. They're pretty wary of government agencies. And all we're asking is to let some of our best bulls hang out around their cows and let nature take its course. We'd only take the F1 hybrid calves for seedstock. Would take no purebred bison calves.

"'Could trademark Purebred Angus Beefalo and defy anyone else to use or equal that brand. Ted Turner's bison are mutts and I can't see any reason he'd ever want to get into beefalo. I'd like to go a step farther and trademark Purebred Western Angus Beefalo too. You can't convince me beefalo pasturing in bluegrass next to a Kentucky racehorse is going to taste anything like range-fed where bison always thrived and our Angus are perfectly suited.'

"Ambrose asked Sid, 'Truck our bulls up there? Or truck bison all the way here and then maintain them until they calve? Damn long drive and we don't have the room. Ranchers around here could get skittish about brucellosis risk. I might be one of them.'

"I said, 'Could always AI them, long as the sire is Angus and the dam is a bison.'"

"Ambrose said, 'Artificial insemination in an open field, now there's a notion. Tell you what, Laura. I think your old testicicle is around here somewhere. You can get your straws from our bulls easy enough if you, um, want to lend a hand. But introducing it to a big ol' bison mama without restraining her, that's what I want to see you do. Here bicie, bicie, bicie.'

"Sid said, 'We wouldn't try to run 'em here. Dad and I have been looking into spreads closer to where the bison are. Located one might work, but it's overkill. Called Crazy Waters Ranch. It's about 8300 acres at the foot of the Crazies. With leased public land it runs over 9,000. Most is conservation easement, a mix of fertile cottonwood bottom land and benches of prairie grass and sage. 300 acres are irrigated. Ranch completely surrounds a 350-acre reservoir with no public access. Ranch owns 150 surface acres of it and the rest is on leased BLM land. Six and a half miles of Sweet Grass Creek runs year-round through the middle of the ranch, with pivots and ditch irrigation from the lake and the creek. People currently leasing are carrying about 300 cow-calf pairs year-round with room for more in the spring and summer.'

"Ambrose asked, 'House on it or just bare land?'

"'Four or five and a bunkhouse. Only interior pictures I've seen are the main house up on a bluff looking out on everything. Logs and stone, twelve thousand square feet give or take, looks like no expense spared. Heated outdoor pool. The other buildings I dunno. It's a working ranch. Probably benefit from indoor renovation. Could always turn it into a destination guest ranch. Market the whole concept. Beefalo on the hoof, their environment. Ranch operations. Beefalo beef itself: its health benefits, the animal science behind it. The lifestyle, the location of the place, the private lake with a dock. Horse tours. Room to roam. Hunting and fishing.'

"'Hotel Turner,' my mom Ruby said. 'Sounds snooty.'

"'Good distance for the luxury trade from the Hyalite/Yellowstone airport—not too far and not too close. Hunting season could rake it in. Game, waterfowl, upland game birds all on the ranch. Official game preserve on part of the land adds thirty days to the season, private access from the ranch only.'

"'Always good to have options. No problem hiring building trades out of Hyalite. If only someone knew a builder with luxury home experience could design and budget and manage. Anyone? Laura? Anyone?'

"'Can we afford it?' said Ruby.

"Dad spoke up. 'We'll see if it makes sense to look into it further. First things first. We'll invite the Assiniboine leaders and ranch managers down here for a tour. See if they like how we do our thing and how well we might get along. We'll do 'em up right. Then we'll pay a visit to the Crazy Waters ranch alone while the tribal council meets.

"'But before we get to any of that, Laura, I'd like you to research the whole beefalo genetics thing and report back with what you find out and what you still need to find out. I'm sure you'll see things we haven't, for better or for worse. Or see deeper into things we're already looking at. Do a high-level risk analysis and a first stab at a risk/reward matrix if you have time, just to give us a decision-making strawman.'

"I'm on it,' I told them. 'How 'bout we meet tomorrow an hour before dinner for a deep dive?'"

# CHAPTER TWENTY-FOUR

## MOMMY THING

Brendan, Hattie and the widow Vanderkaden sat comfortably arrayed in their usual places facing Branch and the fireplace blaze. Behind them in the dining room the Bouvier and the German Shepherd pup eyed bits of leftover food, waiting for table scraps.

The living room was a mess, furniture pushed back from a table saw, sawdust only half swept up. Yesterday Brendan and Branch had finished reroofing, and this morning started ripping out moldy living room drywall. Took it down to the studs and stuffed in insulation. By unspoken agreement Brendan paid for materials while Branch supplied the expertise. Now one long wall was sheathed with blue-streak beetle-kill pine while planks were stacked ready for tomorrow.

Evenings after dinner Branch read aloud from journals, old newspaper articles and books about the mere quarter-century when fur trappers and explorers roamed the Rockies before hordes of settlers ended the era forever. For the last couple of months he'd been concentrating on Hugh Glass, best-known of his time but, now, not as much as Jim Bridger, Kit Carson, John Fremont, Jedediah Smith and John Colter. Or even that thieving bastard John Fitzgerald and made-up characters like Jeremiah Johnson.

Branch took them through the primary sources—George Yount, Hiram Allen, a guy named Dutton—before tackling twentieth-century retellings by historians like John Myers Myers. Most told the same Hugh Glass tale in slightly different ways. The near-fatal bear attack. His betrayal by men he thought he could trust. The miles he crawled before he could walk. Tracking down Bridger and Fitzgerald to get back his knife and his rifle. It boiled down to not much more than a revenge-obsessed victim story.

The room sat captive through it all except a seemingly endless epic poem with lines turned every which way so the couplets rhymed.

"Make it go away," Hattie said when it got too gay for her. "Too twisted."

Branch chuckled. "The story or the English?"

"What English?" said the widow Vanderkaden, who rarely offered more than a grunt. "Guy wrote that's a German. Only ones make sentences like that." Her parents had suffered greatly during Nazi-occupied Holland's Hunger Winter famine. Not much forgive and forget in her.

Branch finished the Myers chapter about Hugh Glass's early years as a pirate and his barefoot trek up to Kansas. It was early and Hattie was holding up as well as anybody could expect, so they sat around talking later than usual.

"Wasn't like that," Brendan said. "He made that up."

"Myers? He took it from the written records of the time."

"No. Hugh Glass."

"Why would he lie?"

"S'pose he had his reasons. Could've been the buried treasure."

"What buried treasure?" Branch said.

"One he didn't talk about."

"You know this how?"

"Must be something you read us way back when," Brendan said.

"Never happened. Never had that conversation and it ain't in no book."

"Well, hell. I remember it clear enough."

"My point exactly."

Brendan shrugged. He knew where this was headed. Branch and Hattie took reincarnation for granted, Hattie with the zeal of the convert and Branch church-raised in the belief. It seemed obvious to them that Hugh Glass was Brendan in a past life.

Brendan wasn't willing to go that far. But there's always been some sort of presence inside him that knows things and feels things. Inherited memories and volcanic bursts of energy, in the cage or other primal situations, coming from somewhere other.

"Will you guys ever stop scheming on me with this past lives stuff?"

"Don't have time not to scheme, Brendan. Little work left for me to do. Top of the list is getting you at peace with yourself. It's your spiritual growth I care about. Who but me's gonna prod you down that path?"

Maybe it's her certainty and acceptance, but his inherited memory dreams are getting stronger too. Like what he thinks of as his wet dreams. Not sexual, but dominated by water. They started a couple of months ago: dim, hazy and fragmentary at first. Sailing—he's never sailed—along a coastline, hiding during the day and running without lights at night. Suffused now with dreamdread, a sense of being pursued.

The dream memories are gradually getting clearer and piecing themselves into sequences. Taking a boat up a wide river, not as afraid now. Slogging through a bog in steamy weather under trees he's never seen before that drip with moss.

Lowering a heavy iron kettle into what must be a swamp. Hanging onto a rope as it sunk into the water, slowly paying out the line. Jumping back as a snake came right toward him. The only poisonous snakes he's ever seen are rattlesnakes. This was something different. Surprised at Brendan's sudden movement, it coiled different, more defensively, not as if it was going to jump but with its head centered in the coils, thrown back and looking up like a baby bird ready to be fed, except with long, unsheathing fangs and this wide gaping mouth all white inside, like it's saying step on me and here's what you get.

And recently he's started dreaming something about a map. And there's a push to these dreams as if, eventually, they'll be clear enough for him to act. Go wherever it is and see if the other end of that rope is still tied to that underwater cottonwood root system. Swim hand over hand down the soggy rope and hook a cable to the cauldron. Winch it up. That's what the presence wants.

He said to Hattie, "You know I'm half-joking, right, if I whine about all this belief stuff you sling at me. Guess you think it's something I need."

"More'n you know," Hattie said. "Face facts, Brendan. You're like no one else. Knew soon's you started coming up here. All you did when Branch was young. Everything you shared with him. Way you guided him, it was like someone was guiding you."

She paused. Her voice softened. "And when you was the one that was young… What I saw in you then? Well, maybe we'll get a chance to talk about that too."

Brendan said, "We may not be as far apart as I've been letting on. I halfassed believe I inherited old Hugh Glass's memories. You two think I was him a long time ago or he was me before I was, however you see it. I have these dreams and they're getting stronger. Lately there's a boat in a lot of them. I don't know nothing about boats."

Branch and the widow looked at each other and stayed silent.

"Close enough to talk about it with me? You've always shied off."

"Someday."

"Someday soon. Not sure about now."

"Not sure about not now," Hattie said. She gave him a long, deep look.

"Okay, now. Inherited memories is what I think, however that works. Or dream memories. What I don't get is why they're getting more intense."

"Told you. The closer to the end of a life, the stronger earlier lives reach out."

"You think I—"

"Relax, Brendan. You're early on the path. If I told you how vividly I'm reexperiencing my past lives now, it'd take your breath away."

"Do either of you ever once believe something you can prove?" Brendan said.

"If all you believe's what you can prove," Hattie said, "you don't believe much."

"Mom," Branch said. "Tell us about a past life. If you're up to it."

Hattie looked around the room. "You really want to hear it? I can keep it pretty short. Don't just patronize me."

Branch and Brendan nodded.

"Branch, turn off a couple of lights so we're mostly just firelight, okay?"

The widow said, "Not sure I should be here for some séance. Things I could be doing."

"Stick around," Hattie told her. "Could somebody get me a glass of water?"

Branch handed Brendan the vaporizer they were using before he headed into the kitchen.

"This was back when Native Americans—First Peoples—still held sway. I was a spirit guide. A fast, far-seeing young hawk named Pi'ksíí. Indians honored me for my vision and some became my people so I could guide them."

Branch brought her the water.

"One day," Hattie said, "I was flying over a plain so full of bison I couldn't see the grass beneath. A band of Indian People camped nearby. Some on horseback lanced and bow-shot bison enough for winter. Everyone took part in honoring and harvesting the animals, celebrating the bounty. The other bison settled nearby to graze."

"Unafraid?" Brendan said.

"Nothing to fear. The killing part was over. They knew what was going on. So I flew over a ridge to the next valley. Almost as many bison but this time no People. Only a few white men on horseback with big rifles riding through the herd, shooting all they could. The rest stampeded away and kept going until they were out of sight. The white men sawed off just the humps and tongues and rode away, leaving the rest behind to rot, almost enough to feed all our People if they were around.

"Hundreds of scattered bison grazed the next valley until something like a huge iron snake chuffed alongside, breathing fire and smoke. The belly of the snake disgorged horses and hunters to ride them. The rifles were bigger. Once the slaughter was done, the white men galloped back to the snake and leaped their horses into open doorways. The train emptied of many other whites, who severed the tongues and humps of the fallen, and flayed off hides they dragged back and threw aboard. More steam erupted and the thing puffed away west, slowly at first. our People limped out of hiding to salvage what they could. But without horses or travois to carry the meat, they just ate their fill and left the carrion behind."

"Ugh," said the widow.

"I flew over the mountains to a beautiful series of small lakes and meadows, but there were only a few straggling bison, and no other animal bigger than a rabbit for miles. Iron snake after iron snake fumed by filled with white folks, headed for strange-looking settlements all along the snake trail. I could only spot a few People left, half-emaciated, their bodies pocked with sickness sores. Some were falling-down drunk.

"My heart felt too heavy to fly but I made it home to ask my silvertip friend Kiááyo the Elder to call a spirit guide council. They agreed it was prophecy. Birds and small animals would likely survive. But big four-leggeds were no match for white people and their big guns.

"Nobody could think of a solution, so Kiááyo said he'd think on it some. We all agreed saving the babies and their babies yet to come required drastic action. No matter how extreme or painful it would be, doing nothing was out of the question."

Hattie paused. Brendan, Branch and the widow stayed silent.

The big-animal spirit guides met again but I was too little to go. Kiááyo offered them a suggestion but wouldn't tell me what. Only said wolf and bear and bison clans had to live on one way or another.

"A few days later I was coursing above a creek for small prey when I saw a grizzly teaching two cubs how to roll big rocks over and claw up grubs underneath. I could tell the bear didn't yet sense the white hunter I'd seen thrashing up from downstream and downwind.

"As the man grew nearer I circled lower to listen. The she-bear told the cubs to crouch in the brush. Then she said something surprising. "'You cubs stay silent. Don't move till I say. Something's about to happen you won't like. Got to do it so us bears live forever. If you have to go it alone you'll know how. Stay with each other and away from the white man.'

"The bear moved into the clearing. Waited silent and still.

"When the man came around a creekbend and saw her, she reared up on her hind legs.

"He raised his rifle.

"She charged.

"He fired.

"Wounded, she swarmed him. Knocked him over with a single swipe. Then ambled a little ways away and watched him.

"The man struggled back to his feet, spurting blood. He pulled his knife from his belt.

"She charged again to get stabbed over and over. She was stronger. She mauled and fractured him.

"While he lay there, unconscious, she flipped him over on his belly, ripped him open and flung some backmeat in the direction of her cubs. Then she straddled the man. Leaning into him above his gaping wounds, she used her sharp claws to rip open her own chest. Gouts of her blood poured into his back until the cavity filled and her blood started pooling with his on the ground.

"The grizzly dragged herself up, crawled toward her cubs and lay down. Called them to her. Said, 'I'm sorry but it was necessary. I have followed the white man's trail. Now I prepare the way for my children, and their children. The Great Spirit has shown me. A day will come when they will outrun the white man in his own shoes.'"

"That's some story," Brendan said.

"Told you it was vivid," Hattie said. "And sad. But the flying, the soaring, the clear skies and beautiful earth below, I can't tell you how fine it was. How alive it was. And sharing my vision with others."

The room was quiet. Then Branch asked Brendan, "Need me spell it out for you?"

"Spell out what?"

"What she was doing. The she-bear took Kiááyo's advice. Poured her blood into the white man's open veins. Mixed body fluids."

Shuddering, the widow said, "That's sick."

Branch added, "His blood chemistry changed. Old Hugh's part bear from then on. The bear inside him's why they're both inside of you.

Why you are who you are, part mountain man, part bear, part fighter, part the Brendan sitting here."

The widow said, "I don't half believe the cowflop being slung around this room. But I'll tell you one thing for sure. If you think some old man and a bear got in a fight and someways that put the old man inside this scoundrel, I'd say don't you ever look at him? The way he walks. He prowls, those shifty eyes swiveling around. He's not but half-human, you ask me. There's bear there."

After a pause, Branch looked closely at Brendan, trying to make up his mind. "Can I tell mom?" he said.

"Tell her what?"

"What you told me to never tell anybody about."

Brendan paused, considered. "That was a long time ago."

"And I've never said a word. But it would be nice if she knew. I've never seen anything so brave."

"S'pose it can't hurt."

"What's all this mystery?" Hattie said.

"You tell it," Brendan said.

Branch said, "We were camping up in the Bob. I was young. Uncle Brendan told me to secure all the food in this big metal bearvault while he put up the tent. I was stupid. I didn't obey. I kept out a little trail mix for a snack. A grizzly came right up to our campsite. We didn't have a fire yet so there was nothing to stop it."

"I'm glad you never told me, "Hattie said.

"What'd the big man do?" said the widow.

Walked right between the bear and me. Roared at me to climb a tree with small limbs and get as high up there as I could. Then stood his ground. The bear started to go around him to get at me 'cause I was running. It was like football. Brendan moved like lightning and blocked the bear. Then they had a staredown, both of them glaring, equals. Brendan's whole posture was different. And, even from up in the tree, I could see his eyes were different. They were animal eyes. And he was so calm. If he was afraid I couldn't tell it. He just stared calmly at that bear, not challenging it or anything. Confident, it looked like, that the bear didn't have a cub there and Brendan did."

"What happened?" Hattie said.

"They kept looking at each other like they were coming to some sort of agreement. And then the griz just turned around and walked off. Didn't look back or nothing. And Brendan gave me pure hell for jeopardizing us. He wasn't mad at the bear but he sure was mad at me."

The widow said, "Some hero. Go back to that other bear and the mountain man."

Brendan said, "No bear would do something like that. Never happen."

"Wouldn't if Kiááyo hadn't come up with the plan. Advised her, grizzly to grizzly, and she followed instructions. I was there. She propagated her bloodline beyond just her cubs. Knew how to hand off her genes to a new host though it killed her. Surrendered the fight but won the war. Cubs might be her last pure bear descendants but her line lives on strong. Whether they's bears on the outside or not. All the way down to you."

Brendan said, "Maybe it's just I'm a fighter, but who'd die for something like that?"

Hattie gazed over at Branch. "I would, for one. It's a mommy thing."

Brendan said, "In an emergency, sure, save your cubs. But not just step up and kill yourself."

"Somebody scared of death might see it that way. But no fear in her. Nor in me."

Her voice faded to a whisper Brendan couldn't catch.

Branch jumped up. "You tired, mom? Help you to bed?"

"Not just yet, son. But thanks. Turn off the rest of the lights, would you, and the two of you go someplace else? My boyfriend here and I ain't done talking."

Branch and the widow gave each other a look and left the room.

Hattie said, "Come sit next to me on the couch, Brendan. So we can look at each other in the firelight."

He did.

In the husk of a voice she had left she said, "Lick me clean, Brendeen. Lick me clean."

He held her. Licked her forehead, her cheeks and her hair. Licked her ears and her neck. Licked her wrists and her hands. Lick, lick, lick.

"You're clean, Hattie darlin'," he said. "Clean as can be."

Peaceful, she died the next afternoon.

The funeral at the Church Universal and Triumphant was surprisingly upbeat. Membership was way off from its heyday but most of the people still there were old-timers who held Hattie in high regard. One thing Brendan had to give them: they weren't hypocrites. They really believed in all that stuff about rebirth and karmic ascension, plus a lot of things they talked about that Brendan couldn't make heads or tails of.

But it got pretty somber once they were back in Pony. Branch and Brendan were trying but it was hard not to mope around without Hattie.

The widow Vanderkaden stayed on, cooking and cleaning. But she was more openly scornful of Brendan.

Branch just ignored the insults. Brendan started wondering did Branch have a mommy thing of his own going on.

Brendan called Natty. Said, "Start booking me some fights." He worked hard to finish up construction projects around the ranch. Without saying anything about it, Branch took the hint and they got things pretty well wrapped up for a while.

Natty came through with a California fight. Just enough time for a good training camp.

He told Branch in private. Branch said the widow'd be leaving soon too.

Brendan said he'd return after the fight. Goodbyes were muted. Seemed as if nobody had much to say.

# CHAPTER TWENTY-FIVE

# RIFLE

Old Glass catches another bullboat ride, this time down the Platte. He's hot on Fitzgerald's trail. Disembarking, he takes off overland back toward Fort Kiowa where the culprit's now said to be.

Going to be a long damn walk but his legs'll get him there. Maybe slower'n he'd like but still. Give him time, put together a strategy. Fitzgerald's a force to be reckoned with. He'll fight dirty as he can and ain't no slouch.

At the fort Glass learns Fitzgerald's still a hop ahead. Rascal joined the Army. Glass wonders did the bastard get wind he's still alive and on his trail. Why he enlisted? Like as not.

Next morning he's back on the warpath.

Nine months after the bear attack he shambles into Fort Atkinson. Says just the one word. "Fitzgerald."

"In the barracks," says the sentry who leads him there.

Loungers jump to their feet. Struck dumb at first.

Glass doesn't much recognize anybody but they do him. The bear story's been around. Old guy near done in by a grizzly, it's him. Murmurs and stares.

Fitzgerald recognizes him well enough. Rises and lazy says, "Well I'll be. Damned if you don't still look half-kilt."

"Looks is only looks," Glass says. "Young Bridger was kind enough to return my knife. Be obliged to take my rifle back from you."

"Well now," Fitzgerald says, "Got me a mighty fine rifle it's true. Just don't recall it being yours."

"It'n me're known all over these parts," says Glass.

"Anyone in this room vouch for they've seen this old fossil with my stopper?" Fitzgerald says.

Glass scans the barracks. They're all young recruits except one grizzled old captain. "Men who knows me ain't much the joining kind. Tell you what though. I'll say out every inch of her engraving by heart. Then you bring out the piece. Everybody'll see did I tell the truth."

Fitzgerald steps up close under his jaw. "Lot of trouble to go to for an old man like you. Best be on your way."

Glass draws his knife from its sheath and offers it haft-first to Fitzgerald. "Look at it real close. Refresh your memory. See does it go with the gun you've been totin' for less than a year."

"Kiss my ass," Fitzgerald says.

"Day I'm holding my rifle again we're done with each other. Can't ask more than that. Go to hell without my help or I'll assist. Up to you."

"You're twice my age," Fitzgerald says. "Crippled as all getout. You'll take naught from me."

"Can't kill him, mister," the old captain says. "Army man's protected. Murder a soldier it's a hanging offense."

"S'posin' he kills me?" old Glass says.

The captain shrugs. "Self-defense, like as not. You're the one challenging. One with the knife."

"Soon be the one with the rifle too." Glass unbuttons his deerskin jacket. "Can't kill him then I won't." He sets the knife down on a nearby table.

Arms near immobile, shoulders stitched to the bearskin on his back, Glass has to dip his head and shoulders low before he can lift the tendon-strung bearpaw with its three-inch claws over his head. Holds it high for all to see. "Might scratch him up some though, he comes at me. You okay with that?"

"No brandishing weapons inside the fort," says the captain.

"Take this knife, you," says Glass to Fitzgerald. "We'll go outside and I'll get it back from you presently. Last used it against the ol' she-bear whose paw I'm 'bout to engage you with. Won that fight but 'twas a real hard win. See how she plays out this go-'round." He rakes the air with the bearpaw.

The old captain says, "Take it to the parade ground, boys. Bare fists. Leave your weapons here. Including that damn backscratcher."

"Part of my clothing," Glass says. "Stays with me always. Earned it."

"Take it from you myself if I have to," the captain says.

Outside Fitzgerald sheds everything but military-issue boots and trousers, and squares off against Hugh Glass in deerskin leggings and buffalo moccasins.

Glass stalks Fitzgerald, who dances away laughing at the shambling old man so stitched up he can only raise one fist at a time.

For months Glass had been giving this considerable thought. Work around his limitations. First thing is get inside, no matter what the cost. Helpless if he ain't in close.

The old man charges the laughing soldier. Old Glass weathers blows to the head he can't block. But he gets to where he can fire off low body shots. A few to the kidneys and one to the liver. A hell of a good knee before Fitzgerald recovers with a flurry of punches and steps back out of range.

Each night on the way here Glass liked to test his limits, practice weird moves. Time to try one right now or give up the fight.

He switches to a southpaw stance and plants his lead leg, the one the bear broke. Can't swing it but, planted firm and held rigid, it's strong as a young tree and lets his hind leg do what it wants. He unclenches his fists and slowly moves forward with hands palm-down and open.

"You old fool," Fitzgerald barks. "Go on back. Die somewhere else. Won't sully my hands with you." He slaps his knee and roars with laughter.

With a roar of his own Glass windmills his outstretched arms. He twirls to his right and drives his left leg high in a roundhouse kick that takes Fitzgerald by surprise, the heel catching him hard behind the ear.

It staggers Fitzgerald. But twirling exposes old Glass's pelted back. Fitzgerald pounces. Grabs an elkhide corner. Tears it loose from the shoulderblade.

Incredible pain drives Glass to his knees.

Fitzgerald reaches for the other top corner and yanks it free. Blood streams over the flapping hide. The crowd gapes at exposed thin salmon-colored meat.

Fitzgerald laughs as Glass struggles back to his feet. "Give it up, old man."

But Glass laughs too. Agony be damned. His arms are free now. He flexes them and loops a powerful left at Fitzgerald's temple.

Fitzgerald raises his arm to block it, leaving Glass an opening. He dives under the guard with a right uppercut that snaps the younger man's head back. Follows with a left to the ribs. A knee to the nuts.

Fitzgerald crumples. Glass kicks like there's no tomorrow. Face, body, neck, groin, anything in reach until he's grabbed and pulled away.

"Medics, get Mr. Glass to the infirmary," the grizzled captain shouts. "Do what you can. Quartermaster, unlock the armory. Get that damn rifle. Bring it to my quarters. Rest of you men disperse."

Fitzgerald lies curled in a ball, groaning softly.

"What about him?" asks a soldier walking by.

"Leave him be. Crawl off when he's able."

# CHAPTER TWENTY-SIX

## THE SNAKE

Brendan Glass and Johnny Legal reach the Snake River Gorge right after noon. Brendan grabs his shorthaul radio and says, "Circle the wagons at the Shoshone Falls overlook. It's a popular spot; nobody'll pay us no nevermind."

He's still blown away by the sweatlodge apparitions. He needs to get where he's going and off the road before he can make sense of it all. But the excruciating pain's dissipating fast. He feels lighter and stronger. And a whole lot older.

Once parked and striding along the sheer basalt cliffs in goosedown vests, he and Johnny gaze downriver along the Oregon Trail where he used to whitewater raft Hells Canyon and upriver toward John Colter's old Stinking Waters stomping grounds near Yellowstone. Second-rate historians claimed Colter discovered the geysers but Indians always knew about them. Just didn't want anything to do with the place. Preferred to keep Earth's skin intact. Why they didn't plant or bury anything. Evil spirits prowled underground. Nothing good bubbled up from down there on its own.

This magnificent river deep below near-vertical canyon walls stirs Brendan's blood. Every time one of his road trips reached this stretch of the Snake he transcended a dividing line in his life. South of it, consensus reality, short attention-span fans and announcers and reporters and interviewers, bloggers and gym geeks and suckerfish remoras, 'roid rats and ring sluts, here today and gone tomorrow.

Above the river, real country and real people. Once there he becomes part of the real world again.

Most runs north he'd sit here half a day making that transition in his head. But patience isn't Johnny's strong suit. He's already firing up the U-Haul. It idles while Brendan unlocks Fast Horse and makes his preparations.

Behind the wheel, Brendan visualizes how the afternoon light will fall. Sun in the south this time of year will be over his shoulder, lighting up the Snake and reflecting off the cliffs on the opposite side. It'll edge westward as they drive east, gradually deepening rock shadows, emphasizing rifts and intensifying crevices as twilight draws near.

From the glovebox he takes a bag of new corncob pipes he orders carved with his signature for his fans. He selects one and reaches for an emptied-out lip balm container. From it he takes a fresh Granddaddy Purple indica bud. Squeezed into the bowl, it offers up a glorious floral aroma.

He replaces the lip balm cap, whose slogan reads, "It Soothes. It Heals. It Protects."

Damn straight. Three hits gets him right where he wants to be. He opens the driver door and taps the pipe against the kickpanel. What's left of the toasted bud parachutes into the breeze. He's not one to scorch it down to the stem.

He reaches into his diversionary stash, concealed under a jacket and sweatshirts stacked on the passenger side, and opens a tin of stenchified dimestore pipe tobacco. By way of disguise he sticks a plug of it into the bowl where the bud was, spits on his hands and wipes them dry.

He steps through his preflight checklist. Corncobs back in the glove compartment. Tobacco tin loosely concealed next to a few unopened beercans and softdrinks under the sweatshirts. He's ready to hit the road.

He honks once. Johnny moves out and Brendan swings into chase position behind, pointing toward Shoshone and Bannock country and the Raft River Parting of the Ways where the old California Trail cuts south while the Oregon Trail follows the Snake.

Further along, huge salmon used to pool below American Falls, too high to hurdle. Early fur traders passed through without incident, trading anything they had with the *Akai-deka* salmon eaters for fresh fish most welcome after months of pemmican and forage.

Brendan guides Fast Horse up the Snake past the first of many unannounced wagon train ambush sites toward Massacre Rocks. Served the settlers right, running long prairie schooner caravans through Northern Shoshone fishing and hunting grounds without so much as a by-your-leave.

The sun is dropping fast by the time the two rigs near Fort Hall, the intermountain west's first Indian trading post. From there they'd swing north and follow the Snake a little farther before it looped east and the land turned into irrigated potato farms and other settlement activity. He welcomes driving that part in the dark. He prefers this sinuous gleaming meander along the Snake to be his last daylight image before opening his eyes to a gorgeous Montucky dawn.

A few miles before they reach the trading post and museum Brendan has a flash of recognition. The backs of his eyelids start to glow. This is right where his forebear stopped to provision up on his way to Santa Fe and Taos five years after recovering from the grizzly attack.

Still a bit stoned on top of highway hypnosis and last night's near-death out-of-body experience, Brendan watches another mountain man mind-movie overlaid with just enough pale windshield reflection to steer by.

As usual, old Hugh Glass makes camp far enough away from the fort to avoid the noise and the stink of two-leggeds and to get some elevation. But it's too close to the settlement for much game. So one clear autumn morning the old mountain man treks out of the bottomlands up a promising game trail along a good-sized stream, leading his mule so he can pack out the deer or two he hopes to run across.

An hour later he tops a rise to confront the backside of a silvertip grizzly male upwind just out of rifle range. Not the best eating except for the hump and marrow but he can skin the beast and swap for venison at the trading post.

Glass loops his mule's rawhide lead around a treetrunk, gets low to the ground and creeps to within forty yards. He stops and charges his flintlock. He aims.

The wind shifts direction just as he touches off the black powder. The grizzly reacts instantly to the scent, spinning, ready to attack.

The ball catches the grizzly in the shoulder rather than through the back into his vitals. He's not deterred. He's just pissed off.

No cover to be had except a pair of cottonwood saplings alongside the creek. The good news is they're closer to old Hugh than to the bear. The bad news is they're real small. Good news is they're too small for an adult bear to climb.

Glass drops his rifle on the way so he can reach the trees ahead of the grizzly. He leaps. Cottonwoods don't have low branches but desperation and rough leggings give him purchase. He shinnies up one as far as he dares. The thin trunk feels ready to give way.

The grizzly goes after the rifle first and chews the wood off the stock. Then he rises to full height, big paws clawing at the sapling only inches below old Hugh's feet.

Legs scrunched up and testicles tucked, Glass wishes for a tail to wrap around the swaying sapling.

The beast drops to the ground and backs away. For a moment Glass thinks he's giving up. But then the bear rises again and braces his broad back against the other sapling. He hops on one giant foot while his other three paws push against Glass's perch.

The topladen sapling Hugh's riding bends alarmingly and starts to crack. But the bear isn't centered well on the other cottonwood and slides to the side.

Propelled by his own mighty force, the bear falls and lands hard, all four paws up and waving.

Old Glass can't help himself. He roars with laughter.

The grizzly gives him a bewildered look. Perhaps it's an injured shoulder. Perhaps it's injured pride. He rolls to his feet, nostrils flaring and snorting steam, and ambles away without a backward glance.

Unfortunately, straight toward old Glass's tethered mule.

## CHAPTER TWENTY-SEVEN

# HYBRID VIGOR

Laura picks up where she left off. "The next day," she tells Branch as they sit on her sofa, "we gathered in Mom and Dad's living room, waiting for Ambrose to show so I could report. I was leafing through the *History of the Tumbling E* because it got printed and bound at the last minute and I hadn't had much chance to look it over. It came out nice, hand-tooled and deckle-edged."

"When do I get my copy?" Branch says, hoisting a local version of a Russian Imperial stout.

"Soon's I order up some paperbacks," says Laura. "Leather's way too expensive for us ordinary folks."

"Who you calling ordinary?" Branch says.

"Which one you saying isn't? Once everybody was settled I started in. I'll just summarize since you already know what kind of work I've been doing."

"How 'bout the real summary version. Thumbs up or thumbs down?"

"Well, I was sure pitching it to them but that decision's a ways off. They've only got the one question to answer now: Is this an opportunity we should pursue further. Asking for my opinion wasn't much more'n a sanity check. But you know me. I'll build a complete success story in my head, how everything's going to turn out perfect, no matter how many unknowns I'm speculating on. That's the question I'll be asking you too: do you support us going ahead?"

"If you're expecting an objective opinion from me, you gotta know there's limits how far I can go that way."

"Objective's not particularly what I'm looking for. The whole plan has to work for the Tumbling E, for my family, for advancing the planetary cowherd, sure. But it has to work just as well for us and for you and for me."

"On the same page there," says Branch.

"One area where objective'd be nice, though. Risk/reward analysis. I'm too rose-colored-glasses to be the right person for that. I'll point out the areas of biggest concern but you and others are the ones to evaluate. Big questions and assumptions about things nobody's attempted."

Branch refills Laura's glass of Hyalite APA as she says, "I backgrounded the folks on how we've consistently improved our cowherd by tracking Expected Progeny Difference data for so many generations. Described how the last few years we've worked directly with industry leaders to correlate genomically enhanced EEPD DNA testing with traditional measured EPDs. Gave my opinion how this confluence is a historic event in Animal Science and possibly the most important development ever. I pointed them to our Association website for details and then went through some breeding history of beefalo and bison.

"I suggested they look at YouTube videos to see footage of existing operations. I'll recommend to you what I didn't dare say to them: Someone calling herself or themselves 4footvagina filmed some real eyeopeners. Footage of beefalo, bison hybrids, and cattle peacefully grazing and giving birth alongside each other shows you more than just words about how much easier raising beefalo is than bison. You can see the progressive improvements in appearance and behavior through the three hybrid generations necessary to achieve fullblooded beefalo. It's like time-lapse hybrid-vigor photography. Heterosis in motion. It's phenomenal to watch. You get the hardiness of bison—free-range pasturing year 'round or haying 'em in the winter—along with the ease of raising cattle.

"You hear lots of off-the-cuff testimony from ranchers about the benefits they've experienced since replacing cattle or bison in favor of beefalo. Beyond the nutritional, health and taste advantages of beefalo meat that Sid covered—and there's way more to be said about that—the whole ranching experience is easier. Trouble-free unassisted birthing—no more vet calls or breech births or everted uteruses. Good rich milk production from the Angus side. Shorter, denser pelt makes both winters and summers easier. No animal barns and maintenance necessary. And beefalo inherit bison's preference for grazing self-rejuvenating grasses rather than the slow-to-replace forbs and flowers cattle prefer. Less trashing of the watershed too.

"All in all, I'm surprised that, even on a small scale, so few outfits have switched to beefalo, and almost none at a full-on commercial level. Hard to believe there's nary a beefalo producer at all in Montucky or adjoining states. Where better than native bison habitat that we've optimized our Angus for as well?

"Can't say I have any desire to raise bison themselves, though, even if just for breeding purposes. Check out the video of relocating wood bison in Alaska. Pretty damn industrial operation. Special containers to move 'em, heavy-duty fencing, all that. Seeing one in a squeeze chute'll tear your heart out. Never meant to be. And frankly I think white people's buffalo history, decimating Indians by killing off their food source, disqualifies us from bison ranching. Should be an Indian thing. Sid and Dad's approach of working with the Assiniboine to obtain that critical first cross-bred generation makes emotional as well as practical sense.

"We're probably better off letting the tribal council decide whether we take our best bulls to them to breed or they haul some of their bison cows down to our place. Better and cheaper for us to pasture our bulls short-term with their herd and then haul out all the cross-bred calves once they're weaned. But there may be some sensitivity on their part to whether white ranchers are polluting or contaminating their Indian herds, even though we'd bring out all the cross-bred calves as soon as they're weaned before any unintentional mix could happen. On the other hand, they might not like how long we'd have to keep their females at our place if we went the other way.

"Be easier for everybody if we could use their bulls with our cows but no can do. It's a violent breeding even with AI, which I doubt they're equipped to do. For one thing, that combination usually throws sterile calves whose size would likely kill off at least some of our birthing cows. But breeding our bulls to their cows should give us mostly fertile heifer calves. The F1 male offspring will be sterile, so we'll cut 'em and sell the steers come winter or keep for our own eating pleasure.

"Once we get enough F1 cows, the Indians'll be done with us, which I think is a much easier sell, culturally and politically, than an ongoing dependency. On our own we'll cross-breed our F1 heifers with our purebred Angus bulls to get an F2 generation that's three-quarters Angus. There's other ways to end up with the right 5/8 – 3/8 beefalo proportion, but this is simplest and it makes sense to minimize the bison influence as early as possible. We lose the hump and the shaggy fur right away, and both F2 males and females will be fertile. Milk production and all the other Angus traits we've been optimizing for are as dominant as possible. Far as I can tell from what little data exists, the beneficial heterosis from admixed bison blood is fully established with the initial cross and carries through into the next generation when we breed F1 cows to F2 bulls to get our 'fullblood' beefalo foundation herd. We'll DNA-test 'em all and start tracking their progeny information as if they were Angus.

"Here's where it gets a little tricky. Sid told us the truth, as we know it today, that EPDs are breed-specific and lose their predictive value once you cross-breed. Partly that's because the math of it all compares pedigree data from all progeny each animal sires or bears, as well as from all their predecessors and all their predecessors' collateral relatives and all their progeny against all registered members of the breed. With cross-breeding you lose all the historical information because there's never been a combined Angus beefalo herd to compare against. But the algorithms in EPD calculations rigidly weight all such comparative information and there's no way to factor it out. Same with genomic EEPD data, where DNA pairings in one breed sometimes correlate with entirely different performance traits, or none at all.

"However, this is where I went out on a limb. Said I think there may be a partial exception. Suppose you're cross-breeding a purebred cowherd like ours that has abundant genetic and performance information with a small, homogeneous, purebred bison herd that's had no opportunity to interbreed with outsiders for a century and a half. Even more than the Yellowstone herd, the much smaller Elk Island bison herd in Canada should all be so genetically similar that I suspect you could treat them as if all the bison were genetically the same single animal. Measuring beefalo traits as if they were purebred red Angus and verifying the accuracy of their EPDs with their performance measurements would, I suspect, show some EPDs continue to be predictable as if they were purebred Angus, and some would be remarkably divergent.

"If so, I'm sure I could manually parse out all the divergent data. I'd look for a sire or dam's Angus EPDs that are stable up until the admixture of bison genetics and then jump wildly. We could never muster the serious supercomputer time to analyze and statistically churn out meaningful beefalo EPDs, even if we amassed decades of data. But with the help of a programmer or two, I think I could code up and automate a way to take existing Angus EPDs and discard any divergent data. We'd have a more limited, cleaned up dataset but I think it would still have predictive value. Meanwhile it's a moving target. 15k DNA tests are state of the art now. By the time we have our first fullblood beefalo generation, 50k DNA tests being developed now will be on the market, more than tripling the available genomic EPDs. It's possible we could end up with more beefalo predictability than we have for Angus now.

"I also suspect that, as our F3 beefalo herd continues to interbreed, the higher proportion of Angus genetics will improve the predictability of our Angus-based EPDs. The herd will grow more Anguslike."

"Sounds like a lot of work," Branch says, "Could be a total flop."

"I doubt it. No way I can see it would be any worse than the seat-of-the-pants beefalo breeding so far, which seems to have gone pretty well where neither side of the mix is purebred. And we should still be gathering reliable performance data to optimize our breeding the old-fashioned way."

"Still, big commitment. Sure this is something you want to devote years to?"

"If I'm not going to do genetics for Pfizer, I'm sure as hell going to do it for the Tumbling E. I'd rather contribute to my family than draw a big-pharm paycheck and fluff up my résumé. It's presumptuous to say we'd be pushing the frontiers of science but I think we can. I'm not sure anybody else is even in a position to try, unless some black Angus producer gets hold of purebred bison, understands the technology as well as I do, and has the vision and the resources. Those are big barriers to entry and we'd still get there first."

"Jeez, Teach. You know what I regret?"

"Not sure I want to hear this."

"Regret hardassing you awhile back when you were going on about breeding your own strains of high-CBD pot and I told you how hard it would be to catch up with the seed gurus. I only understood maybe a third of what you just ran by me, and I still wouldn't know an EPD if it bit me on the ass. But I do know sump'n about F1s and F2s and all of that, and you're so far deeper into it that my money's on you."

"On us too. There's a lot in it for you. We pick up a spread like the one Sid described, you could construction-manage all building improvements if it's needed. My folks hinted pretty broad we need your knowledge and skills. The Crazies are close enough from here or from Pony for it to work. You'd make professional money supervising any building or remodeling without having to do the physical labor. We can hire that. And you could still do your growing at your own place without so much financial pressure. You'd be part of the family, which I'd rejoice in. The Tumbling E would fund the whole deal and we'd work side by side a lot of the time both here and there. We could fix ourselves up quarters in one of those ranch houses. Better than any other solution I can think of yet. Unless you have an alternative you'd prefer."

"Got none. Wow. Lot to think about. How'd everybody take what you had to say?"

"I saw a few eyerolls here and there—Ambrose likes to tease—but it didn't discourage anybody that I could see. Another thing I told them is the Canadian First Nations and some U.S. tribes are working on a treaty or, I guess, more like a confederation. Part of the deal is they want to cooperate in repatriating some Canadian bison back home. Hundred and fifty years ago a couple of ranchers acquired bison calves from the Kootenai-Salish the same year—cruel irony—barbed wire was patented. For the next twenty-five years they built up the herd to 300 head, just as cattle ranchers and sodbusters were dividing up and fencing off all the grazing land. The ranchers had to sell out. Teddy Roosevelt asked the U.S. government to buy the herd but Congress wouldn't give him the budget. The Canadian government stepped up and drove the herd overland to Elk Island National Park, up toward Edmonton.

"That's the Elk Island herd I mentioned. They've been there ever since with no exposure to domestic cattle or other bison. Still purebred, with no chance of brucellosis. Way smaller herd than the Yellowstone one the Assiniboine have, so the gene pool should be more nearly identical and my 'one bison' theory ought to play out the way I hope. That's the breeding stock I want.

"If the inter-tribal talks go well, they hope maybe a hundred young bison can be brought back home for the Blackfeet to manage up by Two Rivers. Take a couple of years, I expect, to work out the details and raise the money, but I think we need to go talk to the Blackfeet the minute we decide to take the plunge. See can we partner up early on, offer them resources. They're more challenged than the Assiniboine for good grazing land—likely for money too—so support from us might be welcome.

"The situation is politically kind of different too. Hats off to the First Nations and the tribes this side of the border for cooperating to restore bison to the plains and re-anchor that part of Indian life. But their last involvement with that herd was in 1872. They were offered the responsibility—can't really say ownership—but declined. So it was white interlopers who developed and sold it to a majority-white government, who moved and housed it in a national park that's not really associated with the First Nations, far as I can tell. So I think white participation should be welcome and we can join them at the table for everybody's mutual benefit."

Branch says, "So you really think the Tumbling E might take this new direction? Seems pretty drastic and sudden."

"So far everybody likes it, long as the numbers come out right. How about you? You haven't said so far. Worried you might hate the idea."

"Seems far-fetched but you know the science of it, not me. 'Fraid that's my only risk/reward opinion except there's a lot of money and effort the Tumbling E'd have to pony up, especially if you were to combine that whole destination resort notion."

"We need to check that part out. But financially the ranch is sitting pretty these days and we've got seedstock and people resources too. As ranchers go, we're less conservative and more adventurous than most. We'd monitor day-by-day how the beefalo proposition goes. We could always start selling off animals if it got to looking too iffy, so I think the risk is manageable. Same with the destination resort notion. There's plenty of out-of-state demand for big, well-run ranches, and leasing grazing and hunting rights can keep it afloat until the right buyer comes along. Including the herd would just be a plus."

"Between that and what your education and experience bring to the party, sounds as if the timing's good."

"Seems right, what with Sid's desire for change, Ambrose wanting to move up. Think too they were they waiting for me to get done with school before we could launch."

"Wouldn't surprise me," Branch says. "Way your fan club was talking about you at the anniversary party. Maybe it's less hasty'n it seems."

"May have noticed dawdling's not much of an Engebretson trait. We vaguely toyed with the beefalo idea awhile back but never got too far. Sid and Mom and Dad are always thinking ahead, kicking around some scheme or other."

It's growing dark outside.

Laura says, "How about for you? Any of it seem threatening?"

"Personally? Not as much as any alternatives we've talked about. Emotionally, maybe a bit. I'm so used to being poor lately that the whole deal seems pretty rich for my blood. Don't want to be looked down on."

"Nonsense. You build luxury homes. Got a track record. Tumbling E folks can cowboy up a shed or so but you're in a whole different league. Several people made it clear when I was back there that they'd welcome and be glad to follow your direction. They—should say we—probably need your knowledge and experience more'n you need ours.

"Not more than I need you," Branch says.

"So where do you stand," Laura says, "so far?"

"You all got more at stake than I do, so I won't say it's not for me, much less that it's not for you. Sounds like you might like the challenge. Find it fulfilling if it all plays out."

"Damn if I'm not pleased. Wasn't sure how you'd react. And I really do want to do this if everybody goes along."

"So what happens next?"

"Put it to all the other Tumbling E stakeholders. Unless enough folks object to exploring further, Sid and Dad will head up to the Fort Peck rez next week and invite 'em down for a Grasshopper Valley, see do we have the means and the skill to be good partners. Same time, Dad asked if you and me would head over to the Crazies to take a first look at that ranch Sid mentioned."

Branch says, "No flies on any of you. But I'm about schemed out for tonight, if it's all the same to you. Take it up again in the morning?"

"Absolutely," Laura says, grinning.

"One thing I haven't heard mentioned," Branch says. "You ever actually eat beefalo? Like the way it tastes?"

"Have for years now, off and on. Love it. Family usually buys a quarter or half for the freezer every fall. Maybe a whole carcass if the rancher or processing plant recommends it's an particularly good year. But only way is to drive over toward the coast or down I-15 into Utah; none nearer and nobody ships in bulk. Once we butcher and dry-age it, you'll see it on the dinner table pretty regular. Can't say's there's anybody doesn't like it 'less you overcook and dry it out. Any way you prepare it, it's a faster, lighter prep."

"All the advantages Sid claimed, how come there's no distribution? Bison meat is pretty easy to find in a supermarket. Even American Wagyu. Would seem beefalo'd be more available than them, not less."

"Beats me," Laura says. "Unless it's just the producers are so small they're selling out locally. Or maybe the herds aren't monitored and managed well enough to ensure the strict bovine/bison ratio the USDA requires to certify and roll-stamp 'em as graded beefalo beef. Parentage is pretty anecdotal without DNA testing to tell us just how much of the bison contains bovine genetics, and there ain't much incentive to do that since it lacks predictive value."

"Might could explain it," says Branch. "Any other uncertainties trouble you?"

"I'm not pestered. See it more as an opportunity. But I've never tasted purebred Angus/bison beefalo. Doubt anyone ever has. Could be a black Angus outfit's experimented a little with the cross, but the bison'd still be mutts. I see no indication anybody in the country's tried. Whole world, far as that goes."

"I love the pioneer in you," says Branch.

"Wish I could reach into the freezer, hand you a couple of beefalo ribeyes. Be the perfect way to end the day."

"Well, maybe not end it," says Branch.

"Beginning of the end," says Laura.

"...of the beginning," Branch adds.

"Here's hoping," says Laura.

"Speaking of eating," Branch says. "Does Naked Noodle deliver? Or," with a leer, "do I need to provide?"

Laura says, "Don't think so but I'll call. If not, Sweet Chili does. We could splurge. Celebrate what I hope we're about to set in motion and what I hope you're hoping too. Refresh our memory of the taste of unadorned bison. Get the local salad and maybe the Phad Phed."

"Maybe green or red curry, get one each of bison and duck, just for the contrast."

"Or the drunken noodles, same way."

"Deal," Branch says. "You want to call, ask 'em what's good tonight?"

Laura says, "Sure do. Tell 'em we're comparison shopping so we can augment their menu, offer 'em local custom-cut beefalo in a couple of years. Can't start marketing too soon."

## CHAPTER TWENTY-EIGHT

# THE JEFFERSON

The Snake coils away from the road. Brendan gets uneasy anytime he leaves the river to traverse this honyocker farm-belt. These big hayfields and prosperous little tater ranches speak to hard work and enterprise. He's always had a hunch if he gets busted transporting weed it'll be someplace like this, law-abiding homesteader descendants still enemies years later of explorers living their own rules.

He flips Fast Horse's interior light on long enough to slug down what's left of a two-liter Diet Coke that's been keeping him wired with an assist from some Crave-labeled xCeed packets he stirred in before dark.

So much depends on the building. Retrofitting a century-old structure's going to be touch and go. Maybe he can get Hampton to hire Branch to supervise the remodel. Make it a condition.

Tightsqueeze folks treat their own differently. The first to congratulate you if you succeed. Unsurprised and quick to point out when you don't. Give you that half-proud, half-sad look the same way they glance at headframes standing like tombstones over underground mines like the Tightsqueeze. Brendan's poor dad Aloysius used to say the stope walls were so tight he had to run for the first rough hollow he could squeeze into when he heard blind mules clipclopping his way down the narrowgauge tracks, dragging full orecarts.

The highway crosses the Continental Divide and joins the trickle of Hell Roaring Creek this time of year on its way to the Missouri River.

A smuggler's moon reflects off the surface of the Clark Canyon reservoir as the little caravan passes by Camp Fortunate, where Sacagawea reunited with her Shoshone brother Cameahwait and the pony herd that got Lewis and Clark's Corps of Discovery to the Salmon-eater's wintering grounds just ahead of the snow.

Years back, Brendan used to hunt this highcountry with an out-of-state permit, guided by a family of outfitters raised here for generations. Won't need them again. First thing he's going to do is shitcan his California driver's license. Montucky residency'll mean he can go anywhere he damn well pleases, guided by instinct and old Hugh's recall.

Half an hour later, Brendan whips by the U-Haul and takes the next exit. The parking lot is empty and everything in the tiny one-horse town is shut down tight except for the cardreader gaspump and an outhouse. He turns up his jacket collar against the cold. "Feelin' a bit itchy out here on the interstate," he says. "Road so empty this time of night we look like a convoy. My gut says we two-lane it the rest of the way."

"Go with your gut," Johnny Legal says. "Just tell me where."

"We'll exit twenty, thirty miles up the road and follow the Beaverhead to where the Big Hole joins up and becomes the Jefferson. Some reason we get separated, you bear left anytime the highway forks but stay straight at the light in Twin Bridges. Gets us to Tightsqueeze the back way. If I'm not behind you, find someplace to lay up and I'll squawk you once I reach town."

"Gotcha," says Johnny, and they're off on the journey's last leg.

It's smooth sailing until near dawn south of Silver Star when a pair of bright headlights comes up fast behind Brendan. Must've been off on a side road or a driveway. He slows down to put more distance between him and the U-Haul. Doesn't want to be followed into town where the speed limit'll let the guy come up on them, give 'em both a long look-see.

Anybody but a cop'd use this straight stretch to pass them both. Instead, highbeams light him up and then flick back down. Bad sign.

Brendan slows down some more. So does the car behind.

Another thirty seconds he's gonna have to act. He punches the button that lowers his window.

Nothing changes.

Brendan reaches into his diversionary cache, exaggerating the shoulder dip he knows cops look for, driver going for a gun or stashing something.

Brendan raises the can far enough to see he got a soft drink by mistake. Quickly puts it back and grabs the beer.

Onehanded pops the top. Sloshes his face and sweatshirt and takes a big swig. Swirls it around like mouthwash.

He floors Fast Horse and overtakes the U-Haul, gives the turn signal a single flash and swoops out to pass. An instant later he dives back into his lane.

Continuing to accelerate up a slight rise, he flings his beercan out the window and watches his sideview to see it glint and spin in the U-Haul's headlights.

Sure as you're born, here come the flashing lights swinging past the truck. No siren, a coptrick they use when there's no traffic, see if he even notices.

Brendan signals as he should and pulls gradually over to the shoulder, followed by the patrol car.

The U-Haul disappears over the rise the way he planned.

He's lit up by the spotlight. Nothing happens for almost a minute before the uniform looms up in his sideview. Montucky Highway Patrol. Backlit florid face under red hair. Looks Irish.

A big maglite shines through Brendan's window. "See your driver's license, registration and proof of insurance, sir?"

"Sure can." Brendan breathes at him.

After a slow examination the state trooper says, "You know the reason I pulled you over, Mr. Glass?"

"No, sir, I sure don't. Didn't think I was over the limit. Cruise control's usually pretty reliable."

"Other way around. You were driving pretty slow when I came up on you."

"Sometimes I get tired, fall in behind a big rig while I have me some caffeine and perk back up."

"Caffeine, you say? Sure it wasn't something else?"

"What I intended it to be."

"I'm not following you, Mr. Glass."

"But you was. Whole point. Saw you behind me, thought maybe I'd been drifting. Grabbed at that can of Mountain Dew over there under the shirts."

Cop eyes and maglite beam follow where Brendan's pointing.

"Instead got me a beer I keep handy for rest areas when I can't unwind enough to sleep."

The trooper waits for him to go on.

"Soon's I popped that top, beer sprayed all over me. Could just see myself smelling of it with an open container and a cop on my ass. No offense, sir. Tossed it. Just wanted to get rid of it."

"How much have you had to drink tonight, sir?"

"Just that one big gulp by accident."

"You wouldn't object to a field sobriety test then, Mr. Glass?"

"Not in the least, ossifer."

A different tone. "Mind repeating what you just said?"

"Huh?"

"What you called me just now."

"Uh, I said officer."

"That's not what I heard."

"What I meant, officer."

The maglite roams the carseat. "Mind telling me what that green powder is over there?"

"Green? Oh, that's my Crave. Energy concoction for these long drives."

"How's that work? You snort it?"

Brendan looks incredulous. "Officer, I've never snorted anything in my life. Put it in water or a soft drink for a boost."

"Put that package down please, sir. Mind stepping out of the car."

"Not at all, officer. Can use the fresh air. Help wake me up."

"You're not awake?"

Brendan lurches out. "Yes sir, sure am now. Meant wake me up more."

The trooper glances back at his clipboard. "I notice this vehicle isn't registered to you, Mr. Glass. Belongs to a corporation. Is that your corporation?"

"Vitasparc? Hardly. One of my sponsors. Big in the energy drink business. That Crave I was talkin' about? It's theirs."

"Sponsor you how?"

"Get the Crave name out there in the sports world. Be a poster boy for energy."

The patrolman checks out the driver's license again and gives him a new look.

"I didn't recognize you," he says. "You're Bear Glass?"

"I am, sir."

"I'll be damned. Big fan, Bear. Can I call you that? We TiVo you down at the station every fight."

"Ever'body calls me Bear."

"What is it you're doing here in Montucky, Mr., er, Bear?"

"Moving here if all goes well. Set up an MMA training camp."

"Here?"

"Tightsqueeze."

"Really?" the cop says. "You'll get a big welcome there, Tightsqueeze being a town of scrappers from way back."

"Expect I might, being from there."

"You're a Tightsqueeze kid?"

"Confirmed at Immaculate Conception. Lived in Dublin Gulch my whole life until the mining went away."

"So how is it you pick Tightsqueeze, all the places you've been and could go? Must be more business to be had elsewhere."

"But a better life. An opportunity came up, I jumped at it. A new sponsor's remodeling a building there, real attractive terms. On my way to see is it suitable."

"Well, welcome back to Montucky, Mr. Glass. But what you've committed here is a serious offense. We don't take littering lightly. There's a sizable fine I can't let you slide on."

"I deserve to pay, officer. Absolutely deserve it. Would never've thrown anything out a window, wasn't I found myself suddenly with an open container in my hand."

"Tell me this," the trooper said. "I go back to where you tossed it, and you know I'm going to, am I gonna find anything else shouldn't be there?"

"No sir."

"Certain?"

"Absolutely."

"How about firearms? Any in the car?"

"No sir. All I ever shoot's black powder'n I leave my flintlock up here with my nephew."

"I was to frisk you, anything I'd want to worry about? Something might stick me? Anything you wish you weren't carrying? Best tell me now if there is."

"No sir."

"I'll take you at your word, Brendan. But I can't miss smelling the alcohol on your breath. I've got to give you a field sobriety test. Understand your story but I have to do my job. Drunk and drowsy this time of night endangers our citizens. I'd be remiss—"

"Of course, officer."

"Call me Steve."

"Of course, Steve. What would you like me to do?"

"Stand on one foot. Keep your balance."

Brendan does his t'ai chi White Crane Spreading Its Wings Into Brush on one leg, which everybody says is pretty good for a round-eye.

"Good. Now follow my fingers with just your eyes; don't move your head."

Brendan nails it except for the wink right at the end.

He maybe pushes it a little too far when he has to walk a straight line, each foot directly in front of the other. Brendan channels a tightrope artist without a balance bar, a Wallenda hundreds of feet up in the air with no net. At the end, while Steve's clipping his pen back in his pocket, Brendan chances a standing backflip right at him. Steve's hand dives toward the Glock on his hip before he laughs at himself.

"Got me there," he says. "You need to get back in your car now, Brendan. Based on your, um, performance, we won't need to do the Breathalyzer. And I won't charge you with an open container violation, which I could. But I do need to write you that littering ticket. Got a local address we can mail the appearance information to?"

Brendan gives him Branch's star route.

"You can pay over the phone with a credit card, don't have to appear. Or you can show up in court. I don't suggest you try to contest it. Judge has a thing about californicating Montucky."

"Thanks, Steve. Would never consider it. No desire to look at trash 'n junk on the roadside, mine or anybody else's. You folks keep your highways nice and clean, not like the cities where I been."

"Guess we're about done then, Bear. Hope things work out for you here. We'd like to have you back. Be good for the economy. 'Specially that sad old town. Sign here, please, and initial it here."

Brendan takes his paperwork back along with the ticket that he signs and returns. "Now that's done," he says, "can I give you something to take back to your buddies at the station house? Not a bribe 'cause I already got the ticket. Just promotional materials I carry for fans. That pile of sweatshirts there? They're freebies." He points to the diversionary stack on the passenger seat. "You hand some out I'd be obliged. Prepublicity for HAMMA."

"Hammer?"

"High Altitude Mixed Martial Arts. HAMMA. The training camp I was talking about. Shirts got my mug on the front, list of my fights on the back. Take you a whole box of Large and Extra Large, whatever you can use. Don't imagine you got too many bantamweights on the force."

"Shit, Bear, I'll take you up on that. Boys won't believe it."

"You want, I'll autograph 'em too. Always carry some Sharpies."

"Hell yeah, Bear."

"Do you one better. Got a crime scene camera with a timer on it? Take a few snaps, you with your hand on my head pushing me into your patrol car. Be good for a laugh or two."

"Could get around, some folks wouldn't see the joke in it. Think less of you."

"Let 'em. Good thing about MMA is there's no bad publicity. The badder the better. Just makes me look tougher. Caption it Steve Outpoints Famed Martial Artist, something like that. Or Submits." Brendan gives Steve another wink, having much too good a time.

What else does he need to prove he's back where he belongs? The old him as much as the new.

# EPILOGUE

# TIGHTSQUEEZE

Brendan doesn't catch up to Johnny Legal until Tightsqueeze, where he raises him on the handheld after recrossing the Divide on the old highway. They reconnoiter where Johnny'd tucked himself behind a warehouse supermarket on the outskirts. After a piss and a twelve-pack of Moose Drool to go they ease onto the interstate, head west a couple of exits and then point uptown.

Halfway up the steep hill, Brendan takes a left and follows the U-Haul a few blocks over to the century-old YMCA building. Almost no one out on the streets this early.

Brendan has given Johnny Legal's photos weeks of scrutiny, but the facade is way grander than he expected. Elegantly simple, not your typically ornate Tightsqueeze public building. More of an east-coast classical look, D. C. or New York. Majestically proportioned, stretching an entire block.

The northern sun, low this late in the year, reflects from each of the tall windows in turn as they drive up, flashing into Brendan's eye like welcome beacons.

What a neighborhood. A gloriously restored Art Deco theater is right across the street next to another refurbished theater. Around the corner, well-maintained rubblestone churches, almost cathedrals.

His building—he's already thinking it's his—fits right in. The way the windows are spaced, all six stories must have real high ceilings. And somebody must've shipped those bricks in. They're redder and denser than any around. Crisp strong edges. Every one looks intact. Don't even need repointing.

He pulls a preloaded spermie from his pocket and fires it up.

Johnny Legal hooks the truck down a sidestreet and around the back to a loading dock.

Brendan parks in the alley, jumps out of the car and guides Johnny back to the dock.

Johnny walks to the front of the building to unlock and soon the loading dock door slides upward. Brendan backs the truck up further until it's flush against the building so they're shielded from view. Not that anybody's there to see them empty the U-Haul with hand trucks and dollies.

They work fast and steady for an hour and a half, glad to be moving around after the long drive. Brendan's pain is almost gone and he's limber.

They bring in grow tents to keep the moms separate. T5 fluorescents and metal halide lamps for veg, high-pressure sodium for flowering. Reflectors for both.

Foot after foot of flex tubing for the air pumps. Semi-rigid hose to bring water to and from the hundred-gallon stock tanks Johnny'll use for reservoirs.

Big-bore PVC pipes for passive return lines from hundreds of blue, squared-off deepwater culture buckets. Nested a couple of dozen at a time on a handtruck, they don't look like much. Spread out and hooked up, though, they'll cover thousands of square feet, room after room.

Fittings and airstones galore. An incredible amount of equipment, see it all in one place like this, an industrial factory in kit form. Wouldn't think it'd be so complicated but Johnny knows what he's doing and the best way to do it. His grow partners back in Cali set him up with the best.

"For now just get the weed and the gear tucked out of sight," Johnny says, "so we can drop the truck off before the lot opens."

They pile everything against the long wall of a windowless room once used as a bowling alley, lane markers still inlaid in the hardwood floors. Must be oak, worth a mint down south and perfect for exercise machines. If bowling balls can't dent it what could? He can already see the photo spread in a sports enthusiast magazine.

Brendan stacks identical U-Haul boxes as high as they'll go on the hand truck and wheels them in. Up against the wall, tilt forward and slide out from under, then back to the truck. He's got a rhythm going; it's just another workout until he gets to tour the rest of the building. If it's half as cool as this...

He blades opens a carton on top. It's full of tidy half-gallon glass jars of manicured product. "Where d'you figure for these?"

Johnny points to an open door to the left. "In that room where I'm settin' the flats. It's got a lock."

Turns out it's the half-concealed pinsetter area behind the bowling lanes. The seedlings are protected by stacked bright plastic WalMart minicrates wired with thin battery-powered LED lights.

Johnny starts carefully removing flats from the crates. He arranges each one neatly on the floor in three long rows butting up against old bowling machinery for returning the balls.

Brendan offers to help. Johnny looks at him like, yeah right, and says, "You bring in the heavy stuff. Use the long cart."

Once each flat is unpacked, Johnny dismantles the crates they were in, stacking the lamps in an out-of-the-way corner and nesting crates to the ceiling.

Brendan shuttles in ballasts on the multicart until Johnny slaps him on the back. "Plants survived pretty much intact. Little droopy some of them from the stress but they'll bounce back."

Johnny erects some pressfit PVC tinkertoy frames so he can hang rows of T5s over the flats. He plugs in a power strip and everything lights up. Little leaves seem to beam and gleam.

He grabs a plastic watering can and disappears into the ballroom toward the Restrooms sign. Comes back dripping and says as he passes, "That Hampton's as good as his word. Lot of work done already. I'll give you the ground floor nickel tour now so you can be scheming on your gym. Then we'll drop off the truck before the lot opens up and our suitcases at the old uptown hotel. It's a beauty, by the way, older'n this place. It'll be where you put up important visitors and the press when you've got an event."

"Okay by me."

"Then we grab us something to eat and unwind at the hotel. We'll walk through this whole place tomorrow. You'll have the entire first floor and all of the second except for security offices. We'll patch up the back stairs to the steam room on the third so your jocks will have exclusive access. You can put a sauna in there, anything you need for cutting weight. But the top three floors are strictly off-limits to you and yours. We'll secure the stairs and the elevator once it works again."

Half an hour later, over wop chops and fries in a casual dive, Johnny Legal says, "Whaddaya think? This gonna work out for you?"

"Work out?" Brendan says. "You kidding? That huge room up front at the far end, used to be a library? Big enough for a sparring cage and some seating for gentlemen's club smokers. Maybe members only, cigars and BYOB? All that walnut paneling? Fireplace you could roast a calf in? The chandeliers? Put the regulation cage in the ballroom with TV cameras. Counter's already in for smoothies 'n a juice bar 'n of course the xCeed."

"Get you a liquor license too if you want," Johnny says. "For big events. They're dirt cheap here."

"Put the classes and one-on-ones in that room further back they used as an art gallery. And you see those big bathrooms? That's real marble, man, wall to wall, individual showers as well as the stalls."

"One thing, though," Johnny says. "About your bailing out on me back there? Let's put it behind us. But things won't ever be the same between you and me."

"They already aren't," Brendan says. "Keep our distance. You stay out of my way. I'll steer clear of yours."

Johnny says, "So you're on board with this?"

"If I never go south again it won't be too soon. Maybe get me a dog. Something big can pack his own food. May even see is there a wife out there for me. Anybody looking for that spandex dude best look again. Be just who I am. Who I always was. Bear's in his lair."

# ABOUT THE AUTHOR

Marshall Lewis Gaddis is a writer, musician and actor who appeared in several films by Jon Jost and more recently in *Copper City*, premiering in 2017, from English filmmaker Jason Massot. His forebears include the explorer Meriwether Lewis and the writer William Gaddis. *Forebear* is his first novel.

He received his bachelor's degree with honors from the Writers' Workshop at the University of Iowa, where his thesis advisor, Kurt Vonnegut, provided valuable insights and advice. After receiving an M.F.A. from the University of Montana, he joined the writing faculty—alongside landmark authors James Lee Burke, Richard Hugo, James Crumley, William Kittredge and James Welch—before embarking on a career as a full-time writer, editor, and publications manager. He divides his time between southwestern Montana and San Diego's North County.

marshallgaddis.com
amazon.com/author/marshallgaddis
marshall@gaddis.com
LinkedIn: http://bit.ly/2dwMvDx
facebook.com/lenwatersmusic
twitter: @marshgad

shivareepublishing.com
shivareepublishing@gmail.com

cover art: shannonstirnweis.com